Solo

Also by Clyde Edgerton

Raney
Walking Across Egypt
The Floatplane Notebooks
Killer Diller
In Memory of Junior
Redeye
Where Trouble Sleeps
Lunch at the Piccadilly

CLYDE EDGERTON

Solo

My Adventures in the Air

A SHANNON RAVENEL BOOK

ALGONQUIN BOOKS
OF CHAPEL HILL
2005

ⅠＲ
A SHANNON RAVENEL BOOK

Published by
Algonquin Books of Chapel Hill
Post Office Box 2225
Chapel Hill, North Carolina 27515-2225

a division of
Workman Publishing
708 Broadway
New York, New York 10003

Library of Congress Cataloging-in-Publication Data
Edgerton, Clyde, 1944–
    Solo : my adventures in the air / Clyde Edgerton.—1st ed.
        p. cm.
    ISBN-13: 978-1-56512-426-4
    ISBN-10: 1-56512-426-X
    1. Air pilots—United States—Biography.   2. Air pilots, Military—
United States—Biography.   3. Vietnamese Conflict, 1961–1975—Aerial
operations, American.   4. Novelists—United States—Biography.
I. Title.
TL540.E3734A3 2005
629.13'092—dc22
[B]   2005041094

10 9 8 7 6 5 4 3 2 1
First Edition

For Shannon Ravenel

With thanks to the boys,
Johnny Hobbs, Jim Butts, Hoot Gibson,
John Barker, Jim Schellar, Dave Grant, Butch Henderson,
Lynn Snow, Tom Wright, and Fox Batistini

In memory of
Bill Katri, Danny Thomas, Rick Meacham,
Dick Olsen, and Terry Glavin

And thanks to Louis Rubin; Liz Darhansoff;
Tonita S. Branan; Margaret Bauer;
Rachel Careau; P. M. and Hannah Jones; Tom Purcell;
Sterling and Anita Hennis; my daughter, Catherine;
and especially my wife, Kristina

CONTENTS

AUTHOR'S NOTE

This book is not for flying instruction. Some details—drawn from memory—may be inaccurate. And exceptions surely dot the landscape of my generalities about flight and flying. Those seeking technical accuracy should read the appropriate flight manuals, and for those needing a detailed, enlightened book about how airplanes behave, I suggest the classic *Stick and Rudder: An Explanation of the Art of Flying* by Wolfgang Langewiesche.

Most conversations in this narrative have been re-created from memory. Though all the people are real, most names (and radio call signs) are made up. Some facts may have become slightly distorted by the fog of time.

Many women pilots fly today, but none were present at flying events described in this book, and so none are included here. In any case, I respect women's piloting abilities and significant contributions to aviation.

Solo

INTRODUCTION

YOU STAND AT THE end of a long dining room table that is bare except for a single toothpick lying there in the middle, pointed toward you. The toothpick is a runway—from two thousand feet up. You are alone in a little airplane. You are sweating, just home from your first solo cross-country flight. And as for that toothpick: you must some-how get a big spoon (your airplane) to land on it and stay on it *or you will die.*

I dreamed of coming home from a solo flight soon after I was old enough to look into the sky and see an airplane.

Sometimes a dream's realization falls short of the dream. Occasionally a dream and its realization match, and then we feel lucky.

For me, flying airplanes has trumped any dream of it. I could never have dreamed the hypnotic beauty of a lake of clouds scooting just below the belly of my aircraft, of towering cumulus cloud formations to my left and right. And I have been blissfully alone while flying solo, tucked securely in my protective cockpit, far away up there in a tiny spot in the wide sky, finding a peace that, as the Bible says, passeth understanding.

Aircraft engine and engine instruments have become, along with airframe and landing gear, an extension of my nervous system.

Beneath the exhilaration lies the unforgiving, exact nature of the whole business of flying: a dependence on geometry, on the number of degrees in a turn, on an exact speed and angle as two aircraft join into formation, or on imagined lines drawn through the sky. This dependency calls for skill. Skill brings confidence and security.

I've flown among billowing clouds, alone, in a supersonic jet, run the aircraft up against and through the edge of a cloud at four hundred miles an hour, turned the airplane on its back, cut the power, fallen upside down through vertical halls of air, and then snapped the aircraft upright and added power to climb again.

My almost crazy love of flying led me through Air Force pilot training, to an assignment in Japan, and on to a year of combat missions in Southeast Asia.

Eighteen years later I bought an old wood-framed, fabric-covered airplane. On summer mornings I'd look through the windshield, just ahead, at a dew-covered grass landing strip in the woods—rising to meet my landing gear. The exhilaration was back. I named my airplane *Annabelle*. The name sounded old-fashioned and romantic.

The philosopher in me warns that the thrill of flying airplanes in war should not be separated from the destruction that warplanes and their pilots bring to other human beings. But the writer in me—and the pilot in me—had to try. And in the process, I've knocked around in my mind's back rooms and closets, found old misgivings and worries about my relationship to my own combat flying, and pulled them out onto the porch.

PART 1

(1948–66)

GETTING THROUGH THE INITIAL SOLO

Early Notions of Flying

ON SOME MONDAY AFTERNOONS in the late 1940s, I held a rough canvas clothespin bag for my mother as she gathered stiff, dry clothes from the clothesline. When an airplane flew over, she surely noticed my looking up. The biplanes were my favorites. They seemed to lazy along with a steady gentle-thunder sound through the blue sky. Perhaps she sensed that I longed to be up there; before I was five years old, she had taken me to the airport several times just to see the airplanes and had snapped my photo with airplanes in the background. One day years later, she drove me to the same airport to catch a plane that would take me away to Air Force pilot training and a war. She did not hesitate in granting me leave nor shed a tear that I know of.

Even so, she was, early on, very protective of her asthmatic only child; she kept an eye on me and guided and disciplined me. Her shielding behavior may have influenced my moving away from her toward danger. But—and lucky for me—despite being protective, she pushed me out into the world, out into our backyard, for example, to fistfight a boy who'd just chased me home. She encouraged independence. And perhaps that also enabled my step into the sky.

One day—I was in my forties and she in her eighties—we were talking at lunch. She sat across from me at her kitchen table, her hand resting around a glass of iced tea. She asked, "Do you remember me taking you to funerals when you were little?"

"Sort of."

"People said you were too young, but I wanted you to experience everything. Do you remember me taking you up to see the electric chair?"

"Oh, yes. That's kind of hard to forget."

I was six years old at the time, but it turns out it wasn't the electric chair. It was the chair sitting in the middle of the gas chamber at Central Prison in Raleigh, North Carolina. Not that I was making picky distinctions in those days. Maybe I should be thankful she didn't take me to an execution, though given my early Bible training about crime and punishment, I might have enjoyed it.

As a boy I soaked up the provincial, conservative culture shared by my teachers, parents, extended family, and church. I learned that there was a God, and that he loved America better than he did any other country, and that any country opposing America was evil—and so was everybody in that country. Nobody said those words, but the message was there.

One of my uncles had lost his arm in World War I.

I knew the following numerical facts as far back as I can remember: after being wounded in his arm and legs, he went twenty-four hours without medical attention, seventeen days without a change of clothing.

Two uncles and several cousins served in World War II. A calling to war was high and honorable. The movie star Audie Murphy had been a war hero. So had Ted Williams; he'd been a pilot. The national media depicted pilots from all of America's wars as the most flamboyant of our country's heroes. To me as a boy, that portrayal was compelling.

I toyed with the idea of becoming a fireman, then a doctor, but when I realized I could be a fighter pilot—a war hero flying airplanes—there was (it turns out) no stopping me, especially after I started seeing "the film." It aired on a local TV station just before sign-off at midnight. An F-104 fighter jet (resembling a rocket with short, straight wings) flew through clouds, performing an aileron roll (a complete rollover from right side up, to upside down, to right side up again) and other maneuvers while the poem "High Flight" was read—all this just before the national anthem played in the background. The film centered all my aspirations and hopes about where I'd end up: in a jet fighter cockpit.

My ticket, I discovered along the way, would be the four-year ROTC (Reserve Officers' Training Corps) program at the University of North Carolina. Cadets wore uniforms and marched in drills once a week, took classes in "military science," attended a summer camp after junior year, and on graduation became Air Force officers, though not necessarily on track to be pilots.

Soon after arriving on campus in the fall of 1962, I walked into the ROTC office. A cadet sat behind a desk.

"If I sign up for the program, can I become a pilot?" I asked. (I'd yet to fly in an airplane.)

"Sure. You'll have to pass a few physicals and some academic tests. You got twenty-twenty vision?"

"Yep."

We talked for a few minutes. Then he asked, "Ever had asthma?"

"Why?"

"Because that's the first thing they ask you, and if you've ever had it, you're gone. I've got bad eyesight. That's what stopped me."

A week or so later, I was filling out ROTC forms for those wishing to fly:

HAVE YOU EVER HAD ASTHMA? ___ YES ___ NO

Well, yes, but . . . I checked no. I would lie to fly.

I WAS NOT A HAPPY CADET. The whole business seemed "Boy Scoutie." I earned demerits for not having my belt buckle lined up with my fly. I quickly got into the UNC ROTC marching band—playing trombone—where the military protocol was more friendly. In my senior year I'd be offered a chance to earn my private pilot's license. If I didn't like flying in a small propeller-driven aircraft, or if I was no good at it, the program would allow me to pick a nonaviation Air Force career—but I wanted no part of that.

During my junior year I learned that a former girlfriend

of mine, Ruby, was dating a guy who had a pilot's license. I called her.

"Ruby, would you do something for me?"

"What?"

"Tell your boyfriend I'm an old friend and ask him if he'd take me flying?"

"'Old friend'?"

"Well, you know, whatever. Yes."

"Is that what you want me to do?"

"Sure. I mean, you could go with us. Have you flown with him yet?"

"Yes."

"Was it fun?"

"Sure was."

"Will you ask him? I haven't flown in an airplane yet and I need to find out if I like it or not . . . on account of this ROTC thing."

"Oh, all right."

I met them at Horace Williams Airport in Chapel Hill, and Ruby's boyfriend took us up in a Cessna four-seater.

I sat in the back and watched and listened as he taxied out; then I lifted away from the earth for the first time and felt suspended, completely dependent on the little airplane holding me. Piloting didn't seem terribly complicated.

I'D BE TRAINING AT the Raleigh-Durham Airport, where my mother had taken me all those years before to see my first airplane on the ground. The airport sits on land where my mother and previous generations of her family lived from the eighteenth century until the airport was built in the late 1930s. Less than a half mile from the airport boundary is a family graveyard with twenty-six graves. I've been there almost every year of my life for an annual grave cleaning.

The Cherokee 140 and the Basics

IN THE 1960S, CIVILIAN INSTRUCTORS hired by the government taught ROTC student pilots to fly. Mr. Vaughn (I don't think I ever learned his first name), about fifty, medium build, dyed black hair with a bald spot in back, was in charge of me and several other student pilots. Not an exceptionally able teacher, he was consistent and very safety conscious. Occasionally Mr. Vaughn displayed a sort of self-congratulatory and awkward sense of humor. But only occasionally. In fact, rarely. Maybe twice. He usually seemed a bit nervous, which didn't make me feel at ease. And he sniffed a lot: "If you'll check under here"—sniff, sniff—"you can see exactly how much strut extension is normal."

As we walked out to the aircraft, a two-seater Piper Cherokee, for my first flight, Mr. Vaughn spoke as if he'd said the same thing many times, as he surely had. What he said about the external preflight check held generally true for all the airplanes I'd ever fly. While he talked, Mr. Vaughn held his checklist—a little book—in his hand,

and he insisted on the importance of using the checklist, not memory, so that nothing would be missed. My checklist was open and I was ready to follow along.

I'd studied the Cherokee 140 flight manual the night before, imagining how the real, live airplane would look up close in the morning.

There it sat, waiting, dew on the wings and windshield.

The first preflight went something like this:

1. "Approaching the aircraft, you look for general condition: no flat tires"—sniff, sniff—"no leaks of oil, gas, or hydraulic fluid beneath the aircraft."

2. Mr. Vaughn stepped up onto the wing and opened the cockpit door. "Look inside and be sure there are no keys in the ignition and that all the switches are where they should be. Remember this always: the guy who flew before you"—sniff, sniff (and here he looked at me as if to announce the punch line)—"is the dumbest pilot in the world. He left all the switches in the wrong position. And guess what? He's going to fly *after* you too, so you better leave everything just right for him." I looked in at the instrument panel, which was familiar from my studying. The electric, leather, and fabric smell of the interior masked another faint smell: fear.

3. "Now, back outside." He walked to the front of the airplane, and I followed. "Open the cowling, like this, just like a car hood, and check the oil level and general condition of the engine. No loose wires and so forth. Check here and here." The engine looked very clean. (I didn't think about its operating mostly in the sky away from dirt and dust.) "Close and latch the cowling."

4. "Check the propeller." Sniff. "Nicks in the propeller can really affect performance. It might not seem like they could, but they can." My hand followed his along the smooth edge of the propeller.

5. "Okay—now let's check the extension of the front wheel strut, under here. This is where cushioning comes in on landing. That's about what you want, right there, about four inches. Think of a pogo stick. Hydraulic fluid does that. Does other jobs too, like the flaps, so you look carefully for leaks."

6. "Now check the leading edge of the wing. Strong aluminum like the rest of the exterior. Be sure there are no dents or nicks that might interrupt the smooth flow of air over the wing. You'd be surprised how much drag a little dent or nick can cause."

Mr. Vaughn placed his hand against the leading edge of the wing and walked along sniffing and talking, and I followed, staring at his bald spot, trying to remember as much as possible.

We, the student pilots, were also taking academic classes about flying. One book I did *not* read back in those days is Wolfgang Langewiesche's classic *Stick and Rudder*. But I was absorbing some of its lessons. Langewiesche says,

> Get rid at the outset of the idea that the airplane is only an air-going sort of automobile. It isn't. It may sound like one and smell like one, and it may have been interior-decorated to look like one: but the difference is—it goes on wings. And a wing is an odd thing, strangely behaved, hard to understand, tricky to handle.

I was learning that when moving into the wind, the shape of a wing causes air to rush over its top faster than across its bottom, creating lift, a kind of suction from above. Langewiesche describes it as a pushing from below. As an aircraft reaches a certain speed along the runway, the wind pushes up the wings and the wings lift the airplane right up off the ground and into the air, and generally speaking, as long as the forward speed is fast enough, the airplane is held up in the air by the wings. The faster the forward speed, the more the wing is lifted. The propeller, turned by the engine, is pulling the airplane through the air whether the airplane is on the ground or not. An airplane propeller works, in principle, like a boat propeller. A *jet* airplane is pushed along by a kind of sustained explosion out the rear of the engine.

I'll leave Mr. Vaughn for a minute and explain a few more fundamentals.

To change the direction and speed of an airplane's path through the air, the pilot moves controls inside the cockpit: (1) the stick coming up from the floor (or the yoke on the end of a rod projecting out from the instrument panel), (2) the rudder pedals beneath the feet, and (3) the throttle (usually a lever on a console or a knob located on the instrument panel).

The stick: If the airplane is flying straight and level, then the stick is centered. Move it forward, and the nose drops. Pull it toward you, and the nose rises. Push it left for a left turn, and right for a right turn. In the Cherokee 140, and in most civilian aircraft built since about 1950, a yoke has replaced the stick. The yoke looks like the lower half of a small automobile steering wheel. You turn it left, as you would an automobile steering wheel (instead of moving the stick left), and it causes the left wing to drop and the right wing to rise. You push it forward and pull it back to lower and raise the airplane's nose, just as with a stick.

The rudder pedals: A vertical rudder (like a boat rudder) at the back of the aircraft, located on the back edge of the vertical stabilizer (the part of the tail that sticks up), is controlled by the rudder pedals and sometimes helps turn the aircraft left or right. The rudder can also help control the aircraft at slow speeds.

The throttle: The throttle lever or knob adjusts a valve that helps control how fast or slow you go. Of course, pointing the nose up or down also changes speed, because gravity is always working for you or against you, depending on what is needed.

Sit in the pilot's seat for a minute. If the engine unexpectedly quits while you are high in the air, then point the nose down a little bit and you'll pick up enough speed to provide lift for the wings, and the airplane will fly just fine, though it's gliding downward. The steeper the glide angle, the faster you go. Level out just a foot or so above the ground. (I'm assuming you're over the Nevada salt flats, a wide expanse of hard, level ground.) As airspeed decreases, lift decreases; but you can keep flying just above the ground by steadily increasing back pressure on the stick between your legs. Soon you reach a very slow airspeed and there's not enough lift on the wings to keep you up. You'll touch down gently and roll to a stop. No engine necessary—like a glider.

On the other hand, if you're flying along and the engine quits and you raise the nose or try to hold the nose up and not let it point down, there'll be less and less wind flow under and over the wings, and the plane will get so slow that it finally becomes uncontrollable. This is a *stall,* and after a stall the wings are ineffective, gravity takes over, and the airplane starts falling, regardless of which way the nose is pointing.

You can demonstrate how a wing works by holding your hand stiff and sticking it out the window of a fast-moving automobile, as if your hand were an airplane wing. You've done this before, of course. Your hand is shaped like an airplane wing: flat along the bottom (the palm) and curved over the top, with the edge out front (the index finger) thicker than the trailing edge (the little finger)—a shape that creates lift. When your hand is at just the right angle to the onrushing wind, you feel your hand being lifted. Think of that as the angle at which the wing is fastened onto the fuselage (or body) of the airplane. If your hands were big enough and you could stick them out both car windows and hold them stiffly at just the right angle to the oncoming wind, then at a certain speed the car, with you in it, would lift into the air. But once the car wheels left the ground, the forward speed would quickly drop and you'd fall back to the road.

MR. VAUGHN stopped along the leading edge of the wing. I picture myself, studying my checklist, walking into him.

7. "Stall-warning lever check: Okay"—sniff—"here in the leading edge of the wing is this very small, flat horizontal lever, about the size of a nickle, see? It's loose and it jiggles. Anytime you get too slow and there's not enough wind coming over it"—sniff—"it drops and a stall-warning horn sounds in the cockpit and the red stall light blinks. So you want to be sure this little lever is free to move up and down. Like that. See?"

8. "Pitot tube check." Mr. Vaughn turned to look at me, then looked back beneath the wing, near the stall-warning lever. "It's pronounced PEE-tow. This little blade-like object picks up the wind flow, see. It's hollow." He bends a bit and looks. "The wind flow through there tells your airspeed indicator how fast you're going. So you want to be sure it's not stopped up by a dead bumblebee, or mud, else you won't know your airspeed."

9. "Static port check," said Mr. Vaughn, reading from his checklist. "Here, on this same bladelike device, are several tiny holes not much bigger than pinholes. They're called static ports, and the air that goes into them allows your altimeter to determine air pressure and then tell you your altitude above sea level. Be sure the holes are clear."

Air does not know how high it is above the ground, but it does know how high it is above sea level—and your altimeter records that height. If you're sitting on the ground in Denver, Colorado, the altimeter says you are 5,431 feet up. If you then fly to Death Valley in California and land, your altimeter reads minus 282 feet up.

10. "Now we walk on around to the back part of the wing," said Mr. Vaughn. I followed along. "Near the outer

edge of the wing here is a flipper that moves up and down. An aileron. We move it up and down to be sure it's not binding. When you lift this one, the other one—over there on the other wing—lowers."

At times Mr. Vaughn confused me. But I was hesitant to ask questions. Our relationship didn't allow a casual familiarity. But I knew not to go long without answers to questions. And sometimes after reading a confusing passage in a textbook or manual, I'd have to make my hand into an airplane, fly it around, and think.

Next time you have the window seat on a commercial jet and the aircraft starts a left or right turn, look near the end of the wing along the trailing edge, and see the slightly displaced aileron. The aileron is always raised on the wing that is dropping and lowered on the wing that is rising.

11. "The flaps," said Mr. Vaughn, "are extended down with your flap lever in the cockpit, and they give the wing more lift at slow speeds. But they cause drag at high speeds, so they are only used at slow speeds, usually when landing or taking off. They help you get into the air more quickly and touch down at a slower airspeed. Be sure these rods are in place and secure."

12. "Okay. Main landing gear check." Here Mr. Vaughn squatted near a tire, and I squatted beside him. "The tires should be checked the way you check a car tire—no bald spots, no visible metal along the treads. Then you kick it." He stood and kicked it. Then smiled at me. First smile. "And you check your struts here, just like on the nose gear. We need about four inches of extension."

13. "Okay. Now we walk on to the tail section. This part,

like a sail on a boat but not as tall, is the vertical stabilizer. You just reach up and grab hold of the trailing edge there—the rudder—and move it back and forth to be sure it's not binding anywhere. Go ahead." I could almost feel the cable move inside the hollow body of the airplane, and I imagined the rudder pedals moving in the cockpit.

14. "The other part of the tail section here is the elevator. Looks just like a small wing, designed as one piece, see." Sniff, sniff. He grabbed it. "We can move the whole thing up and down to be sure it's functioning without any binding. When you pull back on the yoke, it pivots and the trailing end is raised into the wind flow. That blows the tail down, and the nose goes up, so you climb."

"Now we check the same things on the right of the aircraft as we did on the left."

MR. VAUGHN HAD MADE clear how the flight controls worked, showing me what caused (1) one wing to drop and the other to rise so that I could turn left or right: ailerons on the outer trailing edge of the wings, operated from the cockpit by the yoke; (2) the nose of the aircraft to rise and descend: the elevator at the tail section, also controlled by pulling the yoke toward you or pushing it away; and (3) the aircraft to go faster or slower: engine thrust, controlled by the throttle.

Lessons

STARTING LATE IN THE FALL semester of my senior year, and through spring semester, Mr. Vaughn and I spent almost forty hours together in the Piper Cherokee 140. Before flying each day, we'd sit at a table and talk about what we were going to do. He'd sniff and hold his hand like an airplane to demonstrate—and as I recall, Mr. Vaughn's propriety made even this kind of gesture perhaps a bit embarrassing for him. I had a notion that he'd been flying a long time and that it was less fun than it had once been.

Early in my training, before soloing but after I was taking off by myself, we were flying along one day when I became aware of a clinking noise that I must have been hearing for some time but ignoring. I looked and saw that Mr. Vaughn was tapping the metal end of my unfastened seat belt against his yoke. I took the belt from him and fastened it around my waist. He didn't say a word, but I could tell he was proud of his method. And it worked. I've never forgotten to fasten my seat belt since. Other things, but not my seat belt.

The Cherokee 140 seemed sturdy and stable. It always cranked as advertised and I came to trust that it would do what I asked of it. Consequently my attention came to rest on what *I* was able or unable to do as a pilot. Worries about aircraft failure receded to the background.

In the air, when demonstrating a maneuver, Mr. Vaughn took control of the aircraft, showed me the maneuver while explaining it, then gave me the controls and let me practice.

After the flight, I'd get a grade: Fail, Fair, Good, or Excellent. I made Goods on the first several flights, even though I felt I deserved an Excellent or two. Mr. Vaughn seemed to have learned the grammar school teacher's dictum of rarely smiling before Thanksgiving. Finally, just before soloing, I got an Excellent.

Along the way, Mr. Vaughn taught me how

To taxi, take off, and land

The Cherokee 140 steers on the ground with a nose-wheel steering button. Depress the button, and the rudder pedals steer the nose wheel.

Taking off is relatively easy. You point the airplane nose down the runway, add power, and use the nose-wheel steering to stay in the center of the runway at first; then as airspeed increases, you revert to the rudder; and then at fifty-five miles per hour you pull back on the yoke so that the nose wheel lifts from the runway. The airplane rolls on a bit and then lifts into the air. If the left wing starts to drop, you bring it back up with a turn of the yoke to the right and a touch of right rudder. The nose is kept in a climbing attitude (but not too steep) with back pressure on the yoke.

Landing is much more difficult. I remember the two of us on final approach the first time I landed. Not much talking going on—we'd been through this quite a few times, first with him flying the whole approach and landing, and later with me flying until close to touchdown, then turning it over to him. As I flew this approach, Mr. Vaughn lightly and slowly rubbed his hands on his knees. I could sense his readiness to grab the controls. I brought the airplane over the runway threshold and then I—tense, neck stretched to see over the nose cowling, holding my breath for touchdown—landed. It was not the best landing ever, but it was all mine.

To fly straight and level

On a clear day the flat line that separates land and sky—the horizon line—is visible way, way out there, all the way around. It's like the line that separates sea from sky, and as you climb higher in an airplane, it does not get lower, as you might think. It stays way out there: you see it over the nose of your aircraft and near each wingtip when you're flying straight and level. It serves as a reference, and I learned to keep the tips of both wings the same distance from that horizon line for straight and level flying, and I also learned where the nose—in straight and level flight—rested in relation to that line.

To plan for wind drift while flying

Wind drift is comparable to a river current taking you across the river bottom while you "sit still." Mr. Vaughn and I would find a straight road on the ground. We'd start following the road. The wind over the ground would be from left to right, say. He'd ask me to make S turns over that road so that the imaginary line our aircraft made over the ground looked like an S with the road splitting it like the two little lines in a dollar sign. The degree of bank in each turn had to figure in wind effect. To make the loops of the Ss approximately equal in size was not easy in a brisk wind.

To remember that "throttle controls altitude; nose controls airspeed"

Instinct tells you to raise the nose if you want to climb, and to put in the power if you want to go faster. Mr. Vaughn's above rule of thumb broke through instinct. In order to climb, simply add a little power and the aircraft takes care of the rest. To go faster, just drop the nose a bit and the aircraft takes care of the rest. Thinking in his terms simplified some finer points of piloting.

To navigate from point A to point B

To understand the weather charts and written forecasts that come to the airport hourly

It was another language—little figures and circles and designs.

To talk on the radio

I learned what to say, when.

To make a level turn, a descending turn, a climbing turn, a steep banked turn

To perform simple aerobatics, like a lazy eight

"Okay now. A lazy eight just draws an eight out there on the horizon with the nose of the airplane. Like this." Mr. Vaughn added power and started a climbing left turn. As if the nose of the aircraft were a giant piece of crayon, he painted a horizontal figure eight along the horizon line far out in front of us. In the middle of the figure our wings were perpendicular to the ground. It was thrilling.

To recover from a stall

As I said earlier, a stall occurs when the airplane, because of insufficient airflow under and over the wings, refuses to fly and starts to fall. The condition of the engine is not necessarily related to a stall. In other words, the engine generally keeps working just fine during a stall.

Picture a paper airplane you've just thrown. It swoops straight ahead and then climbs. But suddenly at the top of its upward turn, it stops and the nose drops. This brief stop is the moment of stall. The paper airplane does not have the power to continue its course, so the nose drops and points toward the ground, and the airplane heads in that direction (or else it spirals or spins toward the ground). Let's back up to that moment of stall. What has been keeping the paper airplane climbing is the speed of the air over the wings, coming from the force of your throw. That throw has caused the wind to push from below the wings and keep the aircraft up in the air, just as your hand stuck out the window of a fast-moving car is pushed upward as long as you keep the same correct angle and the car keeps its speed. When the speed of our paper airplane is low enough, that upward wind push stops. Weight overcomes lift. The moment of stall occurs. The heavy nose falls first (if you've attached a paper clip to it, making it relatively heavy).

It's all clear and fine when you're talking about how it works with a paper airplane, but now sit in the left seat of the Cherokee 140 (normally the seat of the pilot or the student) with me while Mr. Vaughn, in the right seat (the copilot or instructor's seat), takes me through my first stall and stall recovery.

"We'll do a power-off stall first," he says.

We are flying straight and level. He pulls out the throttle knob to idle and we start slowing down, but to keep the nose up he gradually pulls back on the yoke as our speed decreases. (The single throttle was located between us, but we each had a yoke and a set of rudder pedals.) "We'll just let it slow down, but we're going to maintain our altitude as long as we can," he says. Soon we are down to about forty-five miles per hour and the stall-warning horn sounds (sort of like a teakettle), and immediately the airplane starts shuddering and shaking like a car going over a series of potholes. This is a little unnerving.

"There are your stall-warning signs," he says. Mr. Vaughn has pulled the yoke back to his stomach and is kind of wrestling with it to keep the nose of the airplane up and the wings level. Suddenly—with the yoke still back—the left wing drops, and then the nose drops as if a rope holding it from above has been cut. We head almost nose-first

toward the ground. I now get the idea. Mr. Vaughn releases all that back pressure on the yoke as he thrusts the
throttle knob in to 100 percent power, and we pick up
speed quickly. Then he pulls the yoke toward him so that
the nose comes right back up to level. "There we go," he
says. "We caught it, recovered, and didn't lose but about
two hundred feet," he says. "Now you try it."

I practiced power-off stalls several times, awkardly, recovering with as little loss of altitude as possible, and then
we tried power-on stalls. With a power-on stall, the aircraft enters a climb that is steeper than the engine can
maintain. (Imagine starting up a mountain road that is too
steep for your car engine.) The airplane climbs with the
engine at 100 percent power. Speed drops, and at about
forty-five miles per hour the stall warning sound comes on
and the aircraft shudders. The nose is trying to drop, and
I have the yoke back as far as it will go, trying to hold the
nose up. Suddenly a wing falls and then the nose drops as
if somehow released. You're in a stall but your engine is already at 100 percent, so you can't bring that in to help you
recover; you must use rudder and ailerons to get the wings
horizontal to the ground, and as you reach about fifty-five
miles per hour with the nose pointed downward, you can
smoothly but briskly pull the nose right back up to the
horizon again. You've recovered and in the process lost
minimum altitude.

A stall is a clumsy state of affairs—you momentarily
lose control of the aircraft—and Mr. Vaughn was so precise and safety-conscious that his participation in a stall

and recovery seemed incongruous. Nevertheless, we practiced and recovered from many power-on stalls, power-off stalls, and turning stalls.

All kinds of things can go wrong just after the moment of stall, depending on what the pilot is doing with the flight controls (yoke, rudder pedals, and throttle). The pilot may, for example, instinctively pull back on the yoke to keep the nose up, when the nose should be allowed to fall or should even be pushed over so that speed will increase. And in general, the closer to the ground a stall occurs, the more dangerous it is.

Mr. Vaughn and I practiced stalls at high altitudes, of course. We'd name an altitude that we would pretend was ground level. Let's say we chose five thousand feet. We'd pretend we'd just taken off from the ground and then at fifty-five hundred we'd stall our aircraft and attempt to recover from the stall while remaining above five thousand feet.

ON THE DAY I thought I might fly my initial solo flight (usually planned after about nine hours in the air), we took off and stayed in the traffic pattern — the pattern that airplanes fly for orderly landing. We made several touch-and-go landings (as soon as the wheels are firmly on the runway, full power is applied for a normal takeoff).

Then Mr. Vaughn said, "Make the next landing a full stop."

After the next landing, I taxied off the runway and to the flight building.

"Okay," said Mr. Vaughn, "I'm getting out of the aircraft,

and you take it up for a couple of touch-and-gos and then a full stop. Say 'initial solo' on all your radio calls"—sniff, sniff—"right after your call sign."

"Yes, sir."

I sat alone as he walked away, and then I took a deep breath. "Ground, this is Cherokee Six Seven Two Sierra, initial solo, taxi for takeoff." The empty space beside me seemed as big as the Arctic, as silent as snow.

I took off, entered the traffic pattern. On downwind, I looked at a parking lot far below. Sun glinted off a tiny automobile. My mind held panic at arm's length. I knew my procedures, but the runway looked so narrow. I knew that if the approach didn't feel right, I could execute a go-around, which meant leveling off, adding power, and coming around to land again. As I turned to final approach for the first landing, everything seemed normal. "Throttle controls altitude; nose controls airspeed," Mr. Vaughn's mantra, ran through my head. The Cherokee was doing its job. I'd learned that, left alone, it could fly pretty well by itself. I just needed to make the right adjustments: Add a little left rudder and aileron, a bit of power, pick up the left wing a bit, back off on the power. Airspeed is hot; back off the power some more—no, just lift the nose and wait. Things are looking good. Drop the nose a bit; it feels good. Now flare, hold it off, hold it off. The sudden *uurk-urk* of the main wheels touching, the rattling of the empty airframe, the *urk* of the nose wheel. Down. Add power for takeoff.

I put the little airplane down twice more, then taxied in, all by myself, relieved and happy.

Mr. Vaughn was waiting for me in the flight building with a pair of scissors. I pulled out my shirt and he cut off my shirttail, wrote my name and the date on it, and hung it on the wall beside shirttails of those who'd recently gone before me.

I walked out into the sunlight and pumped my fists above my head.

Cross-Country

AFTER TWENTY HOURS IN THE AIR, it was time for me to plan and fly a cross-country trip all on my own. The trip was to Wilson, North Carolina, then over to a small airfield near Fayetteville, and then back home to Raleigh-Durham. I drew a line for the route on a map and marked mile ticks (short dashes) and minute ticks out from the line. The mile ticks, labled, were on one side of the route line, and the minute ticks on the other. Since I was cruising at around one hundred miles an hour and thus over a mile a minute, the minute ticks were farther apart along the route than the mile ticks.

I took off, flew to Wilson, landed, and took off again, having determined that at about eight minutes after my last checkpoint on this leg of the flight I would see the little airport near Fayetteville. What I didn't know was that I'd confused the minutes and miles written on my flight-planning card, a card that summarized the information written on my map. It wasn't eight *minutes* after that last checkpoint that I'd arrive; it was eight *miles*—and *five* minutes.

At about two miles short of my airport (I thought), I started looking, not realizing that it was a mile or so behind me.

I got on my radio and called the airport to let them know I'd be landing shortly.

Nobody answered. So far, no air-to-ground radio call of mine had gone unanswered.

And when I thought the airport should be directly under me, I could see *no* airport *anywhere*. I looked at my map and then back out at the ground. Nothing matched up. I was sweating. I looked from ground to map. There on my map was a racetrack. I looked all about the earth beneath me for a racetrack. None. I searched on the ground out in front of me, looking for anything that resembled an airport. Perhaps I wasn't there yet . . . but . . . okay, okay. I saw a runway—three runways, and . . . I pulled my power back to set up a glide. Thank goodness. Now, Mr. Vaughn had warned me that to the west of the Fayetteville airport was Fort Bragg Army base, but . . . wait . . . were those . . . *army tanks?* Yes! And *big guns!*

I turned east, added power, started climbing, then called the little airport again.

Someone answered!

"Yes, Cherokee Four Four Seven Charlie," said the voice. "Our airport's at eleven miles from the Fayetteville VOR—that's channel one two two—on the one-eight-seven-degree radial."

"Roger," I said.

Of course. That's how I should have been looking for the little airport once I got lost. I tuned in the Fayetteville VOR. An instrument on the panel in front of me would tell me exactly how far and in which direction I was from any station I could pick up. Okay. Okay. Okay. All I had to do was . . .

"Cherokee Four Four Seven Charlie, what's your location?"

"This is Cherokee Four Four Seven Charlie. I'm south of the Fayetteville VOR at, uh, twenty-three miles."

"Roger, Cherokee. Travel inbound toward the station on a heading of about three zero zero degrees, intercept the one-eight-seven-degree radial, head inbound, and at eleven miles out, we'll be under your nose. Give me a call when we're in sight."

"Roger."

I was relieved. The miles ticked down on the instrument that was saving my life. Twenty, nineteen, eighteen. At twelve miles I looked frantically below the nose. Yes, there it was, just ahead!

"Fayetteville," I said into my radio, "this is Cherokee Four Four Seven Charlie. I have your runway in sight and I'm landing. Numbers, please."

"Roger, Cherokee. Landing runway zero niner. Winds zero eight zero at ten. No reported traffic in the area." (The designation 09 refers to the direction the runway is pointed—in this case, east: 090 is east, 180 is south, 270 is west, and 360 is north.)

Before-landing check. Okay. Complete. No rush.

Mr. Vaughn said to fly over the airport to get my bearings before landing.

I looked at each end of the runway below. There was a big 18 on one end and a big 36 on the other. Was I crazy? Was the world coming to an end? There was no runway 09 down there!

"Fayetteville, this is Cherokee Four Seven, uh, Four Four Seven, and I'm—I'm above your airport and I don't see a runway zero niner. I see one eight and three six and . . ."

Then I saw a wide field that crossed the asphalt runway in the middle at a ninety-degree angle. *Of course. Runway 09 is a turf runway.* They can't write numbers on it. I'm okay! Damn, if I just hadn't—

"Roger," the radio said, "Cherokee Four Four Seven Charlie, we—"

"Never mind, sir, I—"

"—have two runways. One is asphalt; one is turf. You will be landing on the turf runway to the east."

I'd never landed on a turf runway. No problem.

I flew the traffic pattern, forgetting that I was landing at a field three hundred feet lower than my home field. I was so high on my first approach that I had to go around. On my second try I landed, taxied in, and finished my after-landing checklist.

When I walked into the flight building, the man behind the counter with the little radio set beside him said, "So, you're Cherokee Four Four Seven Charlie."

"Yessir," I said. "I couldn't get you on the radio for a while."

"Your instructor called and said you'd be on the way. I had to go outside and I guess I missed your first call."

I hadn't known that radios at small airports often go unattended. "Yessir. I need to look at my map and flight plans for a minute. I got lost somehow."

"Happens to the best of us. Probably be a good idea to call your instructor and let him know you'll be a bit late on the trip back."

"Good idea." I was still flustered. This man was so kind—he didn't say anything about the runway mix-up.

I called Mr. Vaughn. He asked no questions when I told him I'd be a little late getting back. It was as if he already knew.

I sat down, studied my plans, and discovered that I'd confused miles and minutes. I've never confused miles and minutes since. And I never will.

I'd thoroughly embarrassed myself in front of the radio operator, so I decided that my takeoff would be impeccable. Surely after all this, he'd be watching.

The preflight checklist for the inside of the airplane is divided into two sections: "Before Taxi" and "Before Takeoff." On the before-takeoff checklist there is an item that says, "Trim: Takeoff Position."

A word about trim. Imagine you're on the Nevada salt flats in an automobile. You turn the steering wheel to the left. You release it and it straightens up by itself. Now suppose you want the automobile to stay in a turn for twenty minutes. Without a trim device you'd just hold the steering wheel in the turn position, exerting pressure on the wheel in order to keep the car turning—and you'd get tired. A trim device (a small wheel or a small movable button, like the one that moves a rearview mirror on a car door) can be set to the right setting, and bingo, the steering wheel will stay where it is (turning the car) without any pressure, whether you're holding it or not. When you pull back on the yoke (or stick), the airplane will start to climb, but you'll have to hold the yoke back to keep the airplane climbing; otherwise, if you turn it loose, the yoke goes back to a neutral position and the nose drops.

If you have a trim wheel, then you can position it to hold the yoke where it is while you climb, and the hands-off position of the yoke will keep the airplane nose up and the airplane climbing without your having to hold the yoke back. That's what trim is all about. It's an aid. Once you want to level off, you'll change the trim back to where it was. Most pilots trim often so that little if any pressure on the yoke or stick is needed for long.

Now, before beginning your takeoff roll, you set the trim so that only a slight pull back on the yoke is necessary to get you off the ground at the correct airspeed. As you gain speed after takeoff, you may have to change the trim a bit, but basically with takeoff trim established you don't have to worry about exerting strong back pressure on the yoke as you lift off the runway.

On this day, on my first solo cross-country trip, I forgot to set my trim to the takeoff position (a potentially dangerous mistake). And it had last been set in a very nose-high position for landing.

I wanted this to be the smoothest takeoff I'd ever made. Mine was the only plane taxiing out, and I knew

Mr. Radio Man was watching me. I looked through my before-takeoff checklist, missing the trim item, and announced on the radio that I was taking off. At airports with no tower, you always look to be sure no one is landing or is on the runway, announce that you're taking off, and go.

I started my takeoff roll. Liftoff is normally at about fifty-five miles an hour. At thirty-five miles an hour, the nose wanted to lift off the ground, but I held it down. I was puzzled. At liftoff I released forward pressure on the yoke, and the nose pitched up at a dangerously high angle. I firmly pushed the nose back to almost level flight.

Mr. Radio Man would have seen my airplane charging down the runway for takeoff, but instead of smoothly flying off the runway, the plane lurched up into the air with the nose far too high, and then the nose suddenly pitched down to a level flight attitude. Awkward at best. Deathly at worst. Funny in between.

Further humiliated, I realized my mistake and trimmed the aircraft. Never since have I forgotten to set takeoff trim. Those cheap mistakes have a way of burning themselves into your brain—seat belt, miles and minutes, takeoff trim.

I landed safely at home, completed my after-landing check, and walked into the flight building. It was late afternoon and I wasn't sure Mr. Vaughn would still be there. He was. Sitting at our table, waiting. No smile, no frown, no nothing.

I told him that I'd missed the airport in Fayetteville the first time around.

No smile, no frown, no nothing.

"Did you learn anything?" he asked.

"Yessir. I did."

"What?"

"I learned not to confuse my miles and minutes."

"Good."

"And to set my takeoff trim."

"Oh. Good."

And that some runways are turf, I thought. And that different airports are at different altitudes.

He filled out my grade sheet. I was expecting a Fair or a Fail. I got a Good.

Having flown with about twenty instructor pilots since Mr. Vaughn, I now realize I was lucky to get him first. He was patient and very safety conscious. And he knew not to overpraise, because overconfidence can kill you. At this stage I was anything but overconfident.

The New War in Asia

AFTER THIRTY-SEVEN HOURS of flying over a five-month period, I was awarded a private pilot's license. It was March 1966, and in a couple of months I'd get my college degree as well. With my private pilot's license I was free to take a passenger into the sky.

"Why, sure," said my mother. At age sixty-two, she had never been in an airplane.

So six days after getting my license, we were off to the airport. A friend of mine, Ronnie Wiggins, was along. The Cherokee 140 was a two-seater. Ronnie would be my second passenger.

Claire, the woman who ran the desk in the flight building, gave me the key to the airplane I'd reserved. Ronnie waited while my mother and I walked to the airplane.

"Clyde, now are you sure about this?"

"Yes, ma'am."

I insisted that she follow me around the airplane as I explained preflight checklist items. She didn't say much.

She seemed a bit preoccupied. After the preflight check, I helped her up onto the wing and into the cockpit. She'd never worn a seat belt, so I helped her get hers fastened.

We took off. I was all talk about what I was doing and why: how the instruments worked, what they told me. I was just getting warmed up when she said, "Son, please don't talk." She grabbed my knee. "And don't make any more of those *turns* unless you absolutely have to."

We flew about thirty minutes. I landed and took my friend Ronnie up for another thirty while my mother waited on the ground. I wonder what she was thinking. This was the summer of 1966. A new war in Southeast Asia had just gotten under way, and within a few months I'd enter Air Force pilot training.

Driving home that day, I asked my mother if she remembered the day she first brought me to the airport, eighteen years earlier—the day my dream started. "Of course," she said. "I wanted to get you out and about. I wanted you to know what was out there. But I do wish you'd kept taking your piano lessons."

PART 2

(1966–67)

AIR FORCE PILOT TRAINING

Laredo

MY FIRST COMMERCIAL JET trip ever was to Laredo, Texas, in October 1966 to begin my year of Air Force pilot training. Vietnam was still a small war and I hoped it would be over before I had my wings.

I checked in on base at Laredo, then walked through a building and out to a waiting phalanx of fifteen or twenty T-38s. I started taking photographs with my nine-dollar Instamatic camera. Photo after photo—from the front, from the rear, from the side, from a forty-five-degree angle off the side. I could imagine no machine more perfect, more beautiful. Its shape shouted all my dreams of flight.

That first night I wrote home to my parents:

Dear Mom and Dad,
Well, I'm settled. Have had no problems what-so-ever.
I flew the "Whisper jet" into Atlanta and then flew

on another Whisper jet into San Antonio. Boy, they are some airplanes.

This morning when I was to leave San Antonio for Laredo, I arrived at the airport 1 hr. + 30 minutes before takeoff, instead of 30 minutes before takeoff. I had forgot to reset my watch.

At San Antonio I met another boy also coming to Laredo and we have been buddying around together— getting clothing, uniforms, equipment, etc.

The land is flat and there are few tall trees. The weather has been very comfortable today, however.

I haven't had a chance to go into town (about 5 miles away).

I hope y'all are making it o.k. without me. I hope you don't worry about me because I'm doing just fine. I have met several seemingly nice boys—all are friendly. I also met one of the instructors and he was very nice.

At supper I talked to a boy who has 6 weeks to go before he's through with his 55 weeks and he said he thinks I'll be able to come home for Christmas. He said he has enjoyed his training, but stressed the importance of studying and not "goofing off."

I don't mean to be bigheaded (and I might be speaking too soon), but after meeting some of the other guys, I think I'll do okay.

I also learned today that if I find I don't like flying I can voluntarily stop on my own accord, but I think I will like it. The planes that I will fly in about 6 months (the T-38s) are simply beautiful.

My first 2 weeks (starting next Tuesday, I think) will

be rather rough as far as physical training is con-
cerned, but things will ease off a bit after that (so I've
been told).

Food is good: $ .40 breakfast, $ .85 lunch, $ .65
supper and all I can eat each meal.

Tomorrow we are talked-to about the following:
training, physical training, personnel and finance, fire
prevention, medical subjects, security and law enforce-
ment, legalities, transportation, etc.

The chaplain talks to us Friday.

Right now I'm rooming with another guy (he's
nice—a little fat guy. I've seen him only briefly) but in
about a week I'll have my own room to myself. In the
room will be, among other things, refrigerator and air
conditioner. One bathroom, consisting of sink, commode, and shower, is shared by every 2 rooms. Also on
each floor there is a lounge with TV.

Well, I'm very tired and will try to get some sleep
now for I must get up at about 6 or 6:30 tomorrow—
have meeting at 7.

Write soon.

Love,
Clyde

(Over)

11:25 a.m. Wednesday (Thurs.?)—next day

Have been in meetings and filling out forms since 7
this morning.

Things so far have been informal, relaxed and
friendly.

I have found out good news about my pay. My gross pay is $451.78 a month. After taxes, etc. are subtracted I will get total of $382.12.

I am getting a $10,000 life insurance policy for $2 (two) dollars per month.

I wonder if my parents ever mentioned the insurance policy to each other. I wonder if they already had feelings, beliefs, and fears about what I considered "a small war."

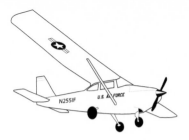

The T-41

THE T-41 WAS THE Air Force designation for a small, slightly modified Cessna 150 airplane much like the Piper Cherokee I'd flown back in North Carolina.

My T-41 instructor was Mr. Washburn, one of the civilians hired to train us at the outset, to weed out the non-fliers. He was only a few years older than I.

Our flight training was from the local airport in Laredo, off base. Every day we'd load up in a bus and head that way. Our training-class designation was 68-C. There were about fifty of us, divided into two squadrons, each with its own set of commanders, pilot instructors, and academic instructors. One group attended academic classes in the mornings while the other group flew. In the afternoons we switched.

We were getting some military training during our flying sessions as well. Besides calling our instructors "mister," we stood at attention when the instructors walked into the room together at the start of each flying day. Our shoes were shined. We weren't allowed to wear boots with our flight suits (drab gray, one-piece suits with zippered pockets here and there on the chest and legs and a small pocket for cigarettes and pencils on the upper left arm) until we flew in the T-37, the little jet trainer we'd fly after finishing the T-41. And after we soloed the supersonic T-38, we'd get to wear a scarf—red polka dots on white for my squadron, sky blue for the other squadron. Wearing the scarf was the last and best uniform change before getting our wings, the silver emblem that we'd wear pinned over the left coat pocket of our dress blues and that would be sewn onto our flight suits in the same place.

We fledglings stood waiting for the bus every day, scarfless, wearing, of all things, plain black shoes, watching other student pilots walk by—guys wearing boots, or boots *and* scarves. We were at the bottom of the totem pole. We weren't even training on base. We had to ride the bus out to the damn *Laredo Airport* every day.

We were graded (Fail, Fair, Good, Excellent) on each flight, and we took academic tests every week or so. Academic subjects included navigation, weather, aircraft systems (the word *airplane* was a no-no), radar navigation, and use of radios.

My training with Mr. Washburn was similar to that which I'd had with Mr. Vaughn, but more formal and structured. And Mr. Washburn, unlike Mr. Vaughn, was athletic, cocky, and a tad sarcastic. He liked to show off.

During an early flight, he set a Zippo lighter on the instrument panel of the T-41. It sat there while he flew straight and level, no problem. Then he started a climbing turn to initiate a lazy eight. If the maneuver is performed correctly, with just the right rudder and yoke movements, then no left or right pressures (slipping and sliding) are felt in the cockpit, and the Zippo stands upright on the instrument panel—even while the aircraft is in a ninety-degree banked, descending turn, that is, with one wing pointed straight down toward the ground as the aircraft falls and turns. Eventually, after several weeks, I could do the same trick. About half the time.

We had a spot-landing contest (to see who can land nearest a painted spot on the runway), and Doug Blockner won it. Doug was clearly the nerdiest of all of us. He was an excellent pilot who'd had lots of flying experience before entering the Air Force. But for some reason he got sick every time he flew in Laredo. I recall walking up behind him out at his airplane one day after we'd each finished a flight. He turned around to say something to me, and all down the front of his flight suit was vomit. Doug was our first "washout," someone who flunked out or left for other reasons—in his case, because of constant air sickness. After him came other washouts, sprinkled throughout our one year of training. I don't remember the exact number of washouts in our class, though we were told that the overall Air Force washout rate in those days was about 25 percent. Some student pilots were unable to do aerobatic maneuvers in the T-37 (loops, aileron rolls, barrel rolls, cloverleafs) and would thus get a string of Fail grades. Others left during spin-recovery training or formation flying. A washed-out pilot usually went to navigator training.

My academic record was good throughout the beginning of pilot training; the multiple-choice tests didn't seem very difficult and my flying grades were high. As we finished our T-41 training, my academic and flying grades put me at the top of my squadron, and it was decided that I and Kevin Boyd, who'd finished at the top of the other squadron, would be on an accelerated program in the T-37. He and I would be flying every weekday in the T-37. Everyone else would be flying every second or third day.

Before we were assigned to a T-37 instructor (an Air Force pilot rather than a civilian pilot) on base, we were each required to enter, of all things, a model-airplane contest. *Required.* The winner would be decided by the T-37 instructors. We were also required to write an essay about why we wanted to be a pilot. These essays, our academic and flight records, and our expertise on the models would help each T-37 instructor decide which student pilot he wanted in his group of four.

My friends started constructing contemporary and classic model fighter aircraft. I went to a toy store. I found a model of a Batplane made famous by the *Batman* TV show. It had four parts, rather than hundreds. It was made for kids. I put it together and entered it in the contest.

I wrote an essay about my dream of flying, about seeing the F-104 on television when I was a boy and hearing the poem "High Flight" in the background. Then I tried to make it funny. I didn't want to be a serious warrior.

Up against the many camouflaged and gunmetal gray model fighters and bombers, the Batplane didn't win, but it provided an opportunity for laughs and conversation, and perhaps caused some resentment here and there. (Our yearbook has a photo of the model aircraft sitting on a table. Someone had removed the Batplane before the snapshot.) The Batplane was—I think, looking back—an outward manifestation of my inner discomfort in the role of warrior. But I would live to learn that a funny warrior is no less responsible for his choice to become a warrior—and is perhaps even more susceptible to dread and regret.

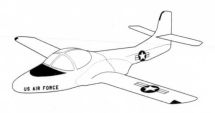

The T-37

MOVING FROM A LITTLE propeller airplane to a small jet trainer was a big jump. So rather than going from one straight to the other, we spent time in a T-37 simulator—a mock cockpit with working instruments. The simulators were all housed in a large room, each one encased in a large box so that once you were seated inside, all you could see were the instruments and flight controls. Our instructors, young airmen or noncommissioned officers (enlisted personnel, not fliers), sat outside the box, at a table with a control panel, while we flew inside in the dark, the glow from the instrument panel against our faces. While one of us flew a simulated mission, an instructor could cause engines to die, fire indicators to light, hydraulic systems to fail. Surely some were happy to watch these young Air Force pilots-to-be sweat and do things like shut down the wrong engine when an engine-fire light came on.

The T-37 instrument panel was significantly more

complicated than the T-41 instrument panel. The T-37 had dual engines; each monitoring instrument had a twin, one reason the panel looked busy.

We attended classroom lectures on the T-37 systems—electrical, hydraulic, air-conditioning and defrosting—on the principles of turbojet propulsion, and on weather, navigation, and other topics. Normally a sergeant lectured using slides of graphs, tables, and charts. Occasionally a lecturer stomped his foot. That meant that what he'd just said would be on the test. Some instructors were just instructors; others were "foot stompers." This was true throughout pilot training.

On the day we were to first fly the real T-37, we were seated around tables, four student pilots per table, in a room with maps on the wall. Our instructors came in; we stood at attention, saluted as our instructor approached. My instructor was a beefy captain who seemed relaxed and carefree (though I was to learn otherwise): Captain Coleman. When he sat in a chair, he leaned it back on two legs. His presence was big. He'd look at you, say something, smile slightly, and raise an eyebrow.

He informed us that each student would normally fly every other day, sometimes every third day, but that I'd be flying every day for several weeks—with another instructor, a Captain Dunning. My initial flying would be accelerated; then I'd be sent back to Captain Coleman. No one mentioned that this was because I'd finished T-41s at the top of my section. (I thought about Kevin Boyd, who'd finished at the top of the other squadron. Before pilot training he'd been a crop duster. His flying abilities were already legendary. He'd had hours of crop dusting and I'd had Mr. Vaughn. Would I be able to keep up with him—to stay at the top?)

We soon learned that the classic Air Force instructor pilot, or IP, expected us to know our stuff, to be over-prepared, and he would *not* patiently guide us through procedures. He wanted to scare us with his strict de-meanor. This was serious business. That's how he had learned. That's how he would teach.

But not so with my new instructor, Captain Dunning, the one who'd have only me as his student. First, he was a bit older that the others. He'd quit the Air Force for ten years—I never knew why—and then reenlisted. At his age he should have been a major or a lieutenant colonel. He was a faithful churchgoer, a Southern Baptist, soft spoken, a bit droopy eyed, and almost constantly smiling. He was an excellent instructor, very patient. He was a Mr. Rogers among Rockys.

Before our first flight, as just the two of us sat facing each other across a table, he explained that we'd be flying together every day, and then he gave a flight briefing, an overview of our first flight. He called the T-37 the Tweet, short for its affectionate name, Tweety Bird, a conse-quence of its small size and the high-pitched sound of its engines.

Before leaving for the equipment room, where we'd pick up our helmets and parachutes, he asked me to re-cite several emergency procedures that we all had to memorize: the correct procedures for responding to an engine failure on takeoff or an engine fire in flight, for example.

And then he did an odd thing. He invited me to his home for supper that evening. I said yes, of course, and then we walked out to the flight line and around our aircraft.

I was wearing boots. Finally.

Captain Dunning talked me through my first preflight inspection, encouraging me to ask questions. I looked down into a cockpit wide enough to seat two pilots comfortably side by side. The wings, large and *not* swept back, would make the airplane easier to fly, more stable than many jets.

Once we were in the cockpit—I in the left seat, he in the right—he said, "Okay now, I'm going to talk you through the starting procedure." I glanced at him. This man was like neither Mr. Vaughn nor Mr. Washburn: he smiled.

The simulator training had been helpful. Though the instrument panel seemed very complex, I'd learned it well.

The crew chief stood in front of us, off to my left. Our glass-bubble canopy was open. We'd lower it while taxiing out to the runway. I could see outside so much better than in the T-41. I was sitting high in the airplane, and the instrument panel was low, rather than almost in my face. When I'd gone through all my checklist items and was ready to start the left engine (the left engine is always started first), I gave a little whirling motion with my left index finger, and the crew chief let me know with the same signal that all was clear. I moved the throttle into idle, pressed the starter button, and checked all gauges—rpm, temperature, oil pressure, and so forth—as the engine came to life. I started the right engine. Even though green lines on the gauges indicated normal parameters, and red lines, danger areas, we were required to memorize and recite normal limits for each instrument.

For the first time, I was about to fly with a fighter-pilot stick grip in my right hand.

Among several buttons and a trigger on the grip was a button that engaged the nose-wheel steering.

The two throttles were side by side on the left console and could be operated simultaneously under my left hand or independently. The instructor had the same setup—stick and throttles.

"Let's taxi," said Captain Dunning.

Through my gloved hands I felt the stick and the throttles that were controlling this machine. I moved the throttles forward. No movement. A little farther. We were moving.

We bounced along the taxiway with the whole world out there. I steered with my feet by pressing on either the left or the right rudder pedal.

Inside my helmet were earphones, and in the oxygen mask covering my nose and mouth was a microphone. My mic and Captain Dunning's were "hot," so that whatever one of us said, the other heard. In order to be heard by someone in the tower, I had to press a button on the throttle grip with my left thumb.

I could look in our rearview mirror and see myself with

my new helmet, sun visor lowered, wearing the oxygen mask now necessary in the T-37.

What was I feeling? A strange pride and power. I saw myself as I thought I'd look to an observer, as I'd viewed fighter pilots all my life—as a hero, with all the attendant awards, recognitions, and love.

While waiting on the taxiway to be cleared onto the runway for takeoff, Captain Dunning said, "Now, when you're cleared on, taxi out and turn around at the end of the runway—as close as you can get to the back edge there, with your nose wheel on the runway centerline. You always want as much runway in front of you as possible."

Cleared for takeoff, I taxied out and stopped the aircraft facing down the runway. I knew what to do, but Captain Dunning would talk me through every move.

"Get on the brakes," he said. "Stand on them if you have to. Now push the throttles to one hundred percent and check all your instruments."

The toes of the rudder pedals operated the brakes. I almost stood on my toes to hold the aircraft still. I brought the twin throttles in my left hand forward and watched the needles on the rpm gauges rise to 100 percent.

"They're all in the green," I said.

"Let's go."

I released the brakes and we were rolling, slowly at first, and then there was a significant pickup of speed. I watched the runway centerline. I was drifting left. I touched the right rudder, too far right, then the left, and was back centered. The airspeed indicator showed 40 knots, 50,

60. At 65 I pulled back the stick, the nose lifted, we rolled along on the main gear, and then the aircraft smoothly lifted into the air. We climbed out at 180 knots, almost twice as fast as I'd ever gone while piloting.

Captain Dunning talked me through climb-out. He made all the radio calls himself so that I would not be distracted. We leveled out at 12,500 feet, higher than I'd ever been as a pilot. I was in a dream.

Before Captain Dunning explained a maneuver, he would take control of the aircraft so I could relax and listen carefully. And when I was taking over the aircraft, I learned to respond to his "You have the aircraft" by taking the stick in my right hand and the throttles in my left and saying, "I have the aircraft," while giving the stick a slight wiggle. The procedure was reversed when he took control. This would be a rule from then on during my time in the Air Force. Side by side we could see each other, but it's easy to imagine the pilot in the front seat of a tandem-seat aircraft saying to the pilot in back, "You have the aircraft," and then turning loose the stick and throttle (without a response) to someone who hadn't heard.

The maneuvers we practiced over the next weeks included stalls, slow flight, steep-banked turns, and aerobatics. We practiced bad-weather instrument approaches to landing, the good-weather traffic pattern, and landing.

After a few weeks of flying it was time for my first check ride. My instructor for that ride was Captain Gillison, from our sister squadron. I felt confident. We flew to our practice area and I performed all maneuvers requested: descending turns, aerobatics, stall recoveries. On the way home he told me to descend. I accomplished my before-descent checklist and started down, looking below me and all around for other aircraft. I'd always been instructed to look out of the cockpit constantly. After I'd descended a thousand feet or so, Captain Gillison abruptly took the aircraft from me. "Edgerton, you didn't do your descending turns." I didn't know what he meant.

Captain Dunning, while instructing me to always be looking outside the aircraft, had not taught me to lower the right wing and then the left as I descended, making gentle turns. This allowed for better vision below the aircraft. Captain Gillison gave me the first of the two Fairs I'd get during pilot training, and it marked my departure from the top of my class. My intense flight training in the T-37, flying every day and preparing for those flights, left less time for academic study, and my academic average would slip, not far; but my stint at or near the top of the class was over.

One day, halfway through a lesson of touch-and-gos, Captain Dunning asked me to land, full stop. It was my day to solo. I taxied to the flight line. He got out of the aircraft and I taxied out, took off by myself, and flew in the traffic pattern for several touch-and-go landings. A traffic pattern flown in good weather (when visual flight rules, or VFR, are in effect) is shaped, looking down from above, like a rectangular racetrack. All turns are normally to the left.

My landing gear is lowered while I'm flying opposite to the direction of landing, with the touchdown point at my nine-o'clock-low position. I lower my landing gear, then my flaps, check to see if my gear-down indicators are in the green, fly straight ahead for a short distance, and then start a descending turn to the left so that a 180-degree turn will put me on a final approach, aiming straight ahead for touchdown. During the final approach, the idea is to get settled down with the right airspeed (slow) and heading so that as I come in over the end of the runway, everything is set for touchdown, and all I have to do is "flare"—that is, pull the nose up slightly so that the aircraft stops descending. As I flare, my throttles are now in idle and I'm pulling back on the stick more and more to keep the wheels barely above the runway. Just prior to stall speed, the wheels settle onto the runway. The trick is to know the exact instant to level off above the runway. You learn that instant by feel. Waiting too long to level off means I bang onto the runway, a hard landing—and perhaps a bounce. Leveling off too high means I float along high above the runway until the airspeed bleeds off and the airplane loses lift and drops way down onto the runway. Another hard landing.

When it's done right, I'll level off just barely above the runway, with a foot or so between my wheels and the asphalt, and I hold it off as the airspeed bleeds, hold it off, hold it off, hold it off, and finally the lowering airspeed (with my throttles in idle) reduces lift, so that just as the aircraft starts to settle toward the runway, why, there's the runway, and the touchdown—at the lowest speed possible, just above a stall—is gentle and smooth. But if the angle down toward the runway is too steep or too shallow, or the airspeed is too slow or too fast, or if I flare too soon or too late—or any combination of the above—then the chances for a smooth landing are reduced.

You know in your muscles and bones if a landing is good, mediocre, or bad—every one, ever. That's one reason I love landing an airplane: feedback is instantaneous and accurate.

Captain Dunning was waiting in the flight building. He shook my hand, patted me on the back. "Congratulations," he said. "Now, I want to talk to you about singing in our church choir." (He was serious.)

AFTER WE'D BEEN flying together for a while, it was time for Captain Dunning and me to fly an overnight cross-country flight. The idea was to plan a flight from Laredo to some other military base in the United States, outside Texas. We'd spend the night and then fly home the next day. Captain Dunning would be along to advise me on all aspects of cross-country flight in a jet.

"Have you ever been to New Orleans?" he asked.

"No, sir."

"Oh, Clyde, you'll love New Orleans," he said, smiling.

After planning for the flight, studying routes and radio procedures, we packed our bags, briefed, and took off. On the way we were supposed to practice low-level navigation.

On the final leg of the journey, Captain Dunning said, "Okay, let's take it down." We were cruising at about 350 miles an hour. I reduced power, and we started losing altitude. At a couple of hundred feet above the ground, I leveled out. We were over a sparsely inhabited area—flat land, large green fields of pastureland. Trees flew by just under us.

"Lower," said Captain Dunning.

I now, just this instant, thirty-seven years later, remember the smell and feel of the T-37—the faint smell of jet fuel, the smell and feel of the cushionlike parachute I sat on, the parachute harness on my shoulders, the worn metal—and there in front of me the crowded, complex instrument panel I knew well. My successes in flying this aircraft, little moments of victory in completing a 360-degree steep-banked turn without losing altitude, loops started and finished at the same altitude, smooth landings—these little victories warmed me to the smells and feels and sights of the cockpit, a cockpit that felt more and more like comfortable old clothes.

With confidence and a thrill, I continued to descend until I was no more than fifty feet above a miles-wide green pasture.

Captain Dunning looked far ahead and said, "Lower. Fly between those two trees way out there."

The trees looked to be about a mile away and I could feel that at my present altitude I'd fly over rather than between them. I pushed the aircraft closer to the green grass of the level pasture, on down until I felt that if I dropped a wing it would scrape the ground. Our speed was over three hundred miles an hour. I was headed right between those two lone trees. They *were* wide enough apart for me to get between them, weren't they? I looked carefully beyond them for a fencerow. Or a cow. I could see nothing but level green earth. I stayed right on the ground. The trees, which had appeared to be moving toward me slowly, were now coming rapidly, and suddenly I was between them and instantly they had jumped far behind me. I'd not looked at the trees; I'd been "feeling" a position exactly between them. And if I'd looked at their tops, I would have had to look up.

This was about the best thing I'd ever done. I had driven a car at age eight sitting in my mother's lap and by twelve had sat behind the steering wheel alone on country roads. And now this. What else could life be about?

In New Orleans we checked into our naval air station barracks, and after dinner, Captain Dunning told me we were going downtown. So I got dressed and we caught a cab for Basin Street. Captain Dunning served as tour guide, but after about fifteen minutes of touring, he said, "Let's go in here."

It was a strip joint.

Captain Dunning was not at all obnoxious about his religion. He generally kept it to himself. But a kind of saintly attitude seemed to define him. He practically always wore a smile. At meals he said the blessing. He never cursed. He'd invited me to attend his church. And I'd sung in the choir!

I'd never been in a strip joint. Well, once or twice at the Durham County Fair back in North Carolina, but that experience was relatively tame.

We were led to a table, where we got our nonalcoholic drinks—I don't remember what they were—or maybe we got whiskey sours. Hellfire, why not go *all the way.*

I was stunned. I looked around, thought about Mrs.

Dunning, about the church we were attending back in Laredo. But not for long.

I can still see the headliner. As I recall, her name was an alliteration, something like Lindy Land. My Lord. She started out wearing a small white outfit, and what she did around the fireman's pole sent golden lust through my blood.

My visual memories of that cross-country trip are two: flying between those trees, and . . . Lindy Land.

Captain Dunning sat silent through the whole show, and when it was over he said, "Well, that was sure something." I was more or less breathless. We left and, in our Christian modesty, never mentioned where we had been, where he had led me. Where I had followed.

The Spin

PICTURE AN AUTUMN LEAF falling from a tree, turning in little circles. That's an airplane in a stall *and a spin at the same time*. Stalls may lead to spins if you don't know what you're doing—or sometimes even if you do know what you're doing.

It is illegal to intentionally spin a civilian aircraft and most military aircraft, but not the T-37. We practiced spins because it's not difficult to accidentally spin the T-37, and we needed to prepare for spin recovery.

What happens at the onset of an accidental spin is that the airplane for some reason gets very slow in the air. Perhaps you are climbing and look back over your shoulder at the ground and forget you're losing airspeed. Suddenly the airplane stalls and begins to shudder. You attempt to turn the airplane, but there's hardly enough wind coming over the wing to act against the raised aileron along the wing's trailing edge. The airplane, now in a complete stall, goes into a lazy turn, but neither wing drops enough to allow the nose to point down far enough for the aircraft to pick up speed and become controllable. So the aircraft starts spinning, like a maple leaf falling to the ground. Or like some paper airplanes after an initial short flight.

During a spin in the T-37, normal movement of the flight controls has no effect. What the pilot must do is "break the spin." To practice, he must intentionally get the aircraft *into* a spin and then recover.

On a typical spin-recovery mission, Captain Dunning and I climbed to above twenty thousand feet for plenty of vertical room. We cinched our seat belts especially tight, stowed checklists, maps, pencils, and any other loose items in our flight suit pockets, and zipped the pockets closed. During the recovery we'd be pulling negative g's, which meant that dirt, coins, pencils, or anything else loose in the cockpit might float up into the air. (Being lifted in your seat in a roller coaster going over a hump is "pulling negative g's." During the stall recovery, something like that happens for several continuous seconds.)

First, Captain Dunning demonstrated the entire process of getting into and out of the spin. He raised the nose, pulled the throttles to idle, and as the aircraft began to stall, he pulled the stick back farther and farther (to hold the nose up). Then, at the last second before a full stall, he popped in the left rudder. (It could as easily have been the right.) The nose dropped, but not much, and the aircraft started a flat turn (little or no bank) to the left and then sped up. Both wings were level or almost level, the nose was slightly down, and we were in a full-fledged spin. What I saw in front of me was the earth moving rapidly from left to right.

This is a condition an airplane will not "fly out" of. Without recovery, it will continue until it hits the ground.

Captain Dunning then demonstrated the recovery procedure while he talked.

"First determine direction of spin. The ground is moving left to right, so we're spinning left. See . . . see, we're spinning left. Keep the stick back in your lap, and apply a very firm full opposite rudder." He *stomped* the right rudder. The whole world out there still moved left to right, but more slowly than before.

"Now we hold the rudder in for one complete revolution. You find a spot out there and wait for it to come back around. That lake and the smoke."

We waited as the aircraft spun.

"Okay, there's the lake. Now, with both hands, *ram* the stick forward as far as it'll go." When Captain Dunning slammed the stick forward to the stop, the nose dipped and we pulled negative g's. We were thrust upward, but our seat belts, tightly cinched, held us down. Dirt and other loose items floated up—a potential hazard, as something could wedge itself into the wrong place and cause problems with the throttle, stick, or rudder pedals.

"If the recovery has been executed briskly," said Captain Dunning, grunting, a bit tense, "the aircraft now enters a controlled spiraling dive, see, gaining speed, and we can bring . . . bring the wings level and then slowly but firmly pull out of the dive . . . There . . . there we go. Add power, and now let's climb back up and you try it. I'll talk you through it. You have the aircraft."

"I have the aircraft."

If we failed at the first recovery—in other words, if we didn't break the spin—then we were to try again. The second of two tries should get us out of the spin before we reached ten thousand feet above the ground. If we tried several times and were still in the spin below ten thousand feet and were not recovering, then the procedure called for us to eject. Pulling the eject handle between my legs would propel my seat and me up through the Plexiglas canopy. The parachute would open automatically and I'd be separated from the seat. At least that's what they told us.

A problem sometimes encountered during spin recovery was determining the direction of the spin. I couldn't be hesitant. During the heat of recovery, I couldn't afford to think this way: If the earth is coming from left to right, does that mean I'm turning left and must press the right rudder? Or does that mean I'm turning right and must press the left rudder? Or the right?

Pressing the wrong rudder would only wrap me more tightly into the spin—as the altimeter rapidly wound down.

To further complicate matters, if somehow in entering the spin the aircraft became inverted, then everything had to be done *backward*. All the lefts became rights and vice versa. And spinning downward, upside down, you didn't want to wait too long to eject—and be propelled toward rather than away from the earth.

During the spin training in the T-37, it was not unusual for a student pilot or two to throw in the towel—wash out—and head for navigator training.

• • •

EJECTION, AS MENTIONED, would send you, in your seat, through the canopy. The seat would break the canopy. Then you'd automatically be separated from your seat, and your parachute would open. If your sitting height was above so many inches, then your head would hit the canopy first and you'd possibly break your neck. So early on, everybody's sitting height was measured. Some guys, shorter than I standing, never made it into pilot training because their sitting height was above the upper limit.

At one point early in our training, before flying in the T-37, we were taken outside to a real ejection seat that had been placed on what looked like a vertical railroad track that ran up to about twelve or thirteen feet in the air. We'd strap in, and a sergeant, standing by, explained the importance of sitting straight up with head back. When one of us got positioned and pulled the handle between his legs, rockets in the seat shot him to the top of the track. We each took a turn. The purpose of the training was to show that there was nothing to be afraid of.

As part of this training we were taught to use a canopy-breaking tool, a device like a hunting knife with a very short blade that, when struck against the top middle of the canopy from the inside, would break the canopy open so that the pilot could climb out of a burning aircraft on the ground. The tool was always in the cockpit. A sergeant demonstrated with a canopy that had been detached from an aircraft. The canopy was propped up and held by one of us so that the sergeant could hit the canopy in the in-side middle and it would shatter—he thought. He tried once, twice, three times, and couldn't get the canopy to break. He gave the tool to one of us, then another, then another. Nobody could break the canopy.

We were told that in some early jet aircraft, you needed to be airborne before ejecting or else your parachute would not open before you hit the ground. In others, you could eject while the aircraft was on the ground, but you needed fifty knots of forward speed. If you ejected before your ground speed was fifty knots, then your parachute would not open before you hit the ground. That was called fifty/zero capability. You needed fifty knots and zero altitude to survive ejection. The T-37 and T-38 had zero/zero capability, we were told.

Somebody raised his hand. "Did the people who designed the seat also design that canopy-breaking tool?"

To prepare for flying with supplemental oxygen through the oxygen mask that we wore in the T-37, we trained in an altitude chamber, a pressurized room large enough for a group of us, in which very high altitudes could be simulated. Let's say I'm flying at thirty thousand feet and I lose my oxygen, but I'm unaware of the loss. The TUC (time of useful consciousness) without oxygen is, as I recall, about a minute. After a minute or so I'll become very confused and then I'll pass out.

Each pilot needed to know his personal signs of low oxygen: tingly feet, tingly hands, numb lips—or something else. The only way to find out was to climb into the chamber and "fly" to thirty thousand feet, lose oxygen, and see what happened.

In the chamber, each of us had an oxygen mask available, but we ascended without it. At thirty thousand feet we were told to pay attention to our symptoms, and when we knew them, to put on our oxygen masks. My lips and fingers tingled. This was my coal miner's bird in the cage.

Then, with oxygen masks on, we were asked for a volunteer—someone to demonstrate what happens when a pilot tries to perform duties without adequate oxygen. I volunteered. I was given a board with square holes and round holes, and, yes, pegs that were round and square. I was asked to remove my mask. I did, and in about thirty seconds I was asked to put the pegs where they belonged, one every second. No problem at first, but then for some reason the people sitting there with masks on were laughing at me. What could possibly be so funny? The peg I held was just dandy for the hole I was staring at, wasn't it?

I was asked to put my mask back on, and I did.

IT WAS NOT UNUSUAL for a student to walk out to an airplane without his helmet or without his parachute, do a preflight, look over the aircraft logs, start to climb into the aircraft, and then suddenly realize his mistake. The instructor never said a word. As long as a student wasn't dangerous, he ate his mistake.

About halfway through my T-37 training, Captain Dunning was assigned to a new student and I was assigned back to Captain Coleman—Mr. Big, my original T-37 instructor, who'd turned me over to Captain Dunning.

Captain Coleman, I'd heard, was a screamer.

On our third or fourth flight, I was flying an instrument

approach. I became preoccupied with my altitude and got off my heading. Captain Coleman suddenly screamed, *"What the hell are you doing, Edgerton?"* He grabbed the hose to my oxygen mask and *squeezed it shut.* I couldn't breathe. He let up, I breathed in, he squeezed it, I couldn't breathe, and he screamed again, *"Can't you hold a god-damn heading and altitude? Good God, Edgerton, where'd you learn to fly? The heading is one eight niner, not one eight six, and you're supposed to be at twenty-one hundred feet. You're two hundred feet low, Edgerton. Are you trying to get my ass killed?"*

My "No, sir" was a "Humph-humph."

I'm glad Coleman wasn't my instructor for spin recoveries.

I asked my friend Cal Starnes, also one of Coleman's students, "Has he got you yet?"

"No way. You got to screw up, and I ain't going to screw up."

A static wire ran from the bottom of the T-37 to the ground while the aircraft sat on the flight line. It reduced the chances of a fire during fueling. The pilot always manually released the wire before he got into the aircraft. One day, Cal overlooked the item on his preflight checklist. He and Coleman got into the plane and Cal started the engines. It was a big, strong wire, clamped to a reinforced grommet in the asphalt, and without its being released, the aircraft would not taxi. Far. Captain Coleman knew, of course, that Cal hadn't released the grounding wire and had motioned for the crew chief, standing by, not to release it — to pretend nothing was wrong.

Cal finished his preflight check, climbed into the aircraft, finished his pre-engine-start checklist and started the engines. He finished his before-taxi checklist and added power to taxi. The airplane moved a foot or so and stopped. Cal increased power. The airplane did not move. He increased power. The airplane did not move.

Coleman reached over and clamped his hand around Cal's oxygen hose. "*What the hell is wrong with you, Starnes? My God, man. Can't you see the airplane is not moving? Can you possibly cut the damn power? What the hell is wrong with you? The airplane is tied to the ground wire, you dummy. Can't you read a simple checklist? Shut down the engine, get out, and release the goddamn ground wire. What the hell's wrong with you, Starnes? Look at your checklist and read how to shut down the damn engines. Now.*" Then he released the hose. Starnes gasped, got his vision back.

A COLONEL NASH, from headquarters, was coming to my squadron to fly with a T-37 student pilot: me. The colonel arrived and we briefed for the mission. This was the highest-ranking officer I'd flown with, and I hoped to impress him.

The preflight—like the preflight of the Cherokee 140—started at the cockpit on the left side and continued to the rear of the aircraft, along the right side, around the front, and back to the starting point. Colonel Nash followed me, watching. Items to check were not unlike those for the little Cherokee 140.

Sheets of aluminum cover the T-37 and are held down with lines of Zeus fasteners (little screwlike devices). On the right side of the fuselage a Zeus fastener was loose. I told the crew chief so that with a little screwdriver-like device he could tighten it.

After I'd completed the preflight and had climbed aboard to sit in the cockpit beside Colonel Nash, I remembered that I hadn't checked to be sure the crew chief had tightened the Zeus fastener. No doubt he had, but I couldn't see it from where I sat. I decided that a visual check—by me—would impress the colonel. As I unbuckled my seat belt, I told Colonel Nash I'd forgotten to check the loose Zeus fastener. He seemed a little impatient but didn't object to my getting out of the aircraft to check. I walked around the front and on around to his side of the airplane. The fastener was tight. I needed to hurry to make the scheduled takeoff time. The crew chief was standing out in front of the aircraft, waiting for engine start. As I hurried around the front of the aircraft—almost in a run—I felt a dull blow to my left leg, just below waist level. What was that? I glanced at the crew chief. His mouth was hanging open. I looked down. The pitot tube, a long pencil-like needle, normally straight out from the nose of the T-37, was pointed off to the left at a sick angle. I couldn't believe it. Now we couldn't fly—not this aircraft, anyway. I looked at Colonel Nash, who was taking off his helmet and rising up in his seat. "What happened?" he asked.

"I walked into the, uh, pitot tube, sir."

"You *what*?"

He was getting out. I'm sure he saw the crew chief's jaw hanging.

The colonel stood beside me.

"I walked into the . . . the, uh —"

"Into the goddamn *pitot* tube."

"Yes, sir. Uh, pitot tube, sir. Yes, sir."

The crew chief ambled up, jaw still hanging.

"We'll have to abort the flight and get another aircraft," said Colonel Nash, looking up to God.

I followed him inside to sign up for another aircraft, and over his shoulder I watched him fill out a form. To understand the significance of what he wrote, you need to know that we'd been warned repeatedly about "bird strikes": while we were flying, a bird might come through the Plexiglas canopy like a cannonball. Pilots had been killed. We were ordered to fly with our helmet sun visors lowered in order to reduce the chance of injury in case of a bird strike.

In the space on his form beside "Reason for Abort," Colonel Nash wrote: "Student strike."

The T-38

EARLY IN THE SPRING of 1967, just as we were getting confident in the T-37, able to "grease on" a landing consistently, it was time to fly the T-38, the aircraft I'd been drooling over since October. And I'd been admiring the scarves worn by student pilots who'd soloed the T-38. White with red polka dots, they weren't scarves in the traditional sense. They were like miniature aprons. A little cloth belt snapped around your neck, and the scarf looped once back underneath and then over in front. Smoothed out, it looked quite natural, very much like a full scarf folded properly. I could hardly wait to have one.

A T-38 instructor worked with four students and would typically fly with a couple of students a day, while the other two students stayed on the ground, studying the T-38 flight manual and academic subjects. We were still spending half a day in the classroom and half a day on the flight line. The academics now covered all the specifics of the T-38: the fuel, electrical, and hydraulic systems, and all the particulars of flying an aircraft far more powerful than the T-37.

Cal, Andy Buckley, Phil Ferguson, and I were assigned to Lieutenant Jackson, a thin, dark, Italian-looking fellow who would fall somewhere between Captain Dunning and Captain Coleman on the "scream scale." He was knowledgeable and precise in the aircraft, as were all our instructors, but instead of screaming, Lieutenant Jackson lectured intensely, either in the air or on the ground. His verbal tone fell between Captain Dunning's sympathy and Coleman's sadism. And he had a sense of humor.

The first ride in the T-38 was called a dollar ride, a tradition, and when it was over, you handed your instructor a dollar.

After a preflight guided by Lieutenant Jackson, I climbed up a ladder into the front seat. A ground crew member followed, helped strap me in, and handed me my helmet. In the T-37 my seat had seemed almost on the ground. Now I was sitting very high in the air, as if I were almost out on the end of a long pole, with no outside reference points. The wings were so far back I couldn't see them without looking over my shoulder.

Lieutenant Jackson climbed into the backseat. He'd be piloting from back there on this ride. I was along only to see what this bird could do. As we taxied out, I thought about how I'd watched pilot after pilot taxi out in the T-38, dreaming of my chance.

Lieutenant Jackson was talking as he taxied us into

position for takeoff. "You're going to feel a little more power here than in the Tweety Bird. Follow through on the controls if you like."

I placed my right hand lightly on the stick grip, my left on the throttles, and my feet on the rudder pedals.

We taxied out and into position on the runway. The throttles moved forward. I felt him on the brakes — as in the T-37, the brakes were under the toes of the rudder pedals. The aircraft, so much newer than the old T-37s, felt clean, tight, and very powerful.

The engines roared as the aircraft, throttles at 100 percent power, held stationary while Lieutenant Jackson checked the instrument readings. This was not a gentle, high-pitched roar; it was a deep, constant thunder. This airplane was almost four times as powerful as the T-37, yet not much heavier.

Lieutenant Jackson released the brakes, and after an initial few feet of slow roll, we began to pick up speed. I felt pressed back in my seat. The throttles went on beyond 100 percent, and the engines roared louder: we were in afterburner (raw fuel is dumped into the burning exhaust for added thrust). Almost before I could think about what was happening, we were airborne, gear up, flaps up. Rather than pulling the throttles out of afterburner and into 100 percent power as usual, Lieutenant Jackson left them in afterburner for a "burner climb." We climbed at a very steep angle.

I'd seen burner climbs from the ground. The aircraft climbs almost like a rocket. I looked outside, down at the earth, which seemed to be shrinking, and then I looked at the altimeter. The altimeter is like a clock (numbered one through ten in a circle) with an hour hand (1,000 feet between numbers) and a minute hand (100 feet between numbers), and the minute hand was making one revolution every two seconds! We'd be leveling off at 15,000 feet *thirty seconds* after takeoff. (That's about 360 miles an hour, measured *vertically.*) Well, this was the most amazing . . . I was itching to fly it.

Just before reaching 15,000 feet, Lieutenant Jackson pulled the throttles out of afterburner. We flew around a bit. He did an aileron roll and a loop. Then he pushed the throttles into afterburner again as he pointed the nose slightly down to pick up speed rapidly. I watched the airspeed indicator. Four hundred fifty . . . 480 . . . 520 . . . 570. I felt a slight bump as the aircraft went supersonic — faster than the speed of sound, a speed at which some experts once believed an airplane would fall apart.

When I was fifteen, I'd counted down, day by day, for nine months until the day I got my driver's license — I was mad to drive. Had I known about this, how long would I have counted? Lieutenant Jackson raised the nose of the aircraft and entered a rapid climb, still in afterburner. The altimeter showed 20,000 , 30,000, 40,000 feet. The sky turned a darker and darker blue. At 52,000 feet the sky was a very deep blue, unlike any sky I'd ever seen. The airframe began to buffet a bit. We were as high as we could go and as high as I'd ever again be from Earth.

A winding-down sound brought my eyes to the instrument panel. The left engine instruments were winding backward. Engine failure?!

"Oh," said Lieutenant Jackson. "I forgot to tell you this might happen. Lack of oxygen. Engine failure. No problem."

We descended to about 30,000 feet on one engine. Lieutenant Jackson told me from the back how to restart the engine up front. "Okay, the left throttle is in idle. Hit the start switch. There you go. Good. We're up and running again." The left engine instrument needles moved until they matched the needles on the right engine instruments.

Then we were on our way home.

"Do you want to fly for a few minutes?" he asked.

"Yessir."

"You have the aircraft."

"I have the aircraft."

Oh, angels. Oh, angels who have visited me. I tried a gentle right turn, then a left turn. "Okay if I roll it, sir?"

"Sure."

I pulled the nose up slightly, snapped the stick to the left, and held it. The aircraft rolled 360 degrees, through inverted, and as it neared upright I centered the stick. I looked out and about and did a clearing turn to be sure no other aircraft was in sight. I rolled inverted, wings level, then pulled back on the stick and performed the second half of a loop. The maneuver is called a split S. Back straight and level, I pushed the throttles into afterburner. We jumped forward, accelerating. What a kick! I rolled it again as I pulled the throttles back out of afterburner. Those two trees on the way to New Orleans were fading into the second row of all-time exciting flying events. Lindy Land lingered.

Lieutenant Jackson took control of the aircraft and we headed home. It was, overall, a relatively short flight because the afterburners consumed so much fuel. Back on the ground and safe inside the flight-planning room, I handed Lieutenant Jackson a dollar bill.

My buddy Cal Starnes was about to fly. He asked how it was. I told him it was about the same as the T-37.

"You lie."

"Naw, I swear. I was expecting something special, but you can tell on run-up that . . . I mean, I don't know if it's the insulation of the cockpit or what, but there is no feeling of power or anything, and then the burner climb-out actually felt slow."

Cal turned his head to the side a bit, tucked his chin, frowned. "Are you shitting me?"

"I'm thinking about switching to helicopters."

A FEW MORNINGS LATER, at 0700, we all sat at tables in the main briefing room. At my table sat Starnes, Buckley, and Ferguson. Our instructors walked into the room. We stood at attention. Lieutenant Jackson approached us and said, "Be seated." On the surface he was all business. Behind the facade was a twinkle in his eye. Looking back, I think the kindness and sentimentality he'd lost in instructor training had been replaced by a kind of nonabrasive, humorous sarcasm.

Jackson would fly with me at 0830 and then with Ferguson at noon while the others studied. After a brief discussion of scheduling and other business, the other pilots left for the study lounge. Lieutenant Jackson and I discussed what would happen during my first instrument ride—the first after the dollar ride. I'd be in the backseat under a hood that extended, accordion-like, just under the canopy and over the entire backseat so that I couldn't see outside, and with the exception of taxi and touch-down, I'd do *all* the flying. Then after weeks of learning to fly on instruments only, I'd move to the front seat and be able to look around.

Lieutenant Jackson asked me a few emergency proce-dures. For example, if he said, "Engine-fire warning during flight," I'd recite, "Throttle-affected engine retard to idle. Throttle-affected engine off if fire-warning light remains illuminated." Then we stopped by the equipment room to pick up our helmets, G suits, and parachutes. A G suit snaps around the waist and legs and inflates when g's are pulled. G's are a measure of gravitational pull. During cer-tain maneuvers (rapid pull-ups, hard turns) the pilot is pressed downward toward the bottom of the aircraft.

It works like this: say the aircraft is cruising at 400 knots. Your body is sitting in the airplane also going 400 knots straight ahead. Suddenly you pull the stick back and the airplane climbs. Your body will want to keep going straight, but since it must stay in the plane, you get pressed against the seat bottom while the airplane makes the tran-sition to a climb attitude. After the transition, the g's stop. Three g's means that if you were on a scale, you'd show three times your normal weight. Vision becomes impaired at around six g's. First comes a gray-out, and then a tun-neling of vision. At seven or eight g's, the pilot may black out, but still be conscious. Beyond eight g's comes unconsciousness, until the g's are released. The inflation of the G suit around the stomach and on the legs causes body fluids to be retained in the upper part of the body, keeping more blood in the head and reducing the chances of a blackout or unconsciousness. High-g maneuvers usually occur during aerobatics and especially air-to-air combat, but not during the kind of flight, an instrument flight, that we were about to take. Even so, we were required to wear G suits on all flights.

Once strapped into the backseat, I lowered my canopy, then reached behind and over my head and grabbed the leading edge of the large canvas hood and pulled it forward until it snapped into place in front of my face, over my head. A fitted partition prevented my seeing outside through the instructor's canopy up front. I made my radio call to ground control for clearance to taxi—Lieutenant Jackson taxied—and then once we were near the runway, I switched to tower control. After we received clearance for takeoff, Lieutenant Jackson taxied out and stopped in the middle of the runway, as near the end as possible. He gave me control of the aircraft. I glanced at all indicators to be sure engine temperatures, oil pressures, and other readings were in the green. I held the brakes with my feet and moved the throttles up to 100 percent and checked instrument readings again while the aircraft shuddered from the power of the racing engines. I released the brakes and slipped the throttles forward into afterburner. I began the takeoff roll on instruments only, watching the heading indicator especially, to keep the aircraft heading down the middle of the runway. There was no very sensitive instrument to keep me in the middle of the runway. However, in bad weather conditions, taking off from the *front* seat, being able to see outside, I'd follow the runway centerline, lit by my landing lights, and I could take off with that outside visual aid and then after liftoff immediately go back on instruments and stay on them until I was above the clouds. But under the hood in the backseat, I couldn't see the runway in front of me, and if I drifted left or right of the centerline, Lieutenant Jackson applied left or right rudder from the front seat to keep the aircraft in the middle of the runway. At 135 knots I began pulling the stick back. All was suddenly smooth; I was in the air. Soon after we became airborne, Lieutenant Jackson pulled up the handle that retracted the gear and then the handle that retracted the flaps, and I felt a pickup of airspeed (because of reduced drag). Things were happening so much faster than in the T-37—so fast that I could barely keep up. At 300 knots I pulled the throttle out of afterburner, keeping the nose at only about a 3-degree pitch up, and suddenly we were at 400 knots. I raised the nose to hold the speed down to four hundred knots for the climb out. Four hundred knots is about 460 miles per hour.

I was supposed to level off at 12,000 feet. In the T-37, in the weeks prior, in order to level off at 12,000 feet, I'd wait until reaching about 11,700 feet and then start smoothly pushing the nose forward (from the climb attitude) while reducing power, so that I'd level off at 12,000 feet. I'd been warned by Lieutenant Jackson to start my level-off a thousand feet early in the T-38. I forgot and shot right through 12,000 feet to almost 13,000 feet. This happened regularly on the first few level-offs in the T-38, much to my embarrassment. I would learn to think several steps ahead of what I was doing. To find myself concentrating on what I was doing at the moment meant I was dangerously behind.

Each time I flew, I learned more about the feel of the aircraft. Remember the first few times you tried to parallel-park a car? You didn't feel as if you were a part of the car. You wanted it to do one thing, but it seemed to have a mind of its own. Once you become proficient at parallel parking, you can better "feel" where the car is, where the curb is. If you have to do it often—say, several times a day—you quickly gain proficiency. You'd get *real* good if you knew that being just a bit off could kill you.

Lieutenant Jackson said, "Okay, Edgerton, let's make a thirty-degree banked turn to the right."

I very smoothly moved the stick to the right so that the right wing dropped and the left wing rose until my angle of bank was exactly 30 degrees. If you lower your arm from straight out so that your hand drops about 2 feet, that is, relatively speaking, about how far my right wing lowered. An instrument on the instrument panel called an attitude indicator—a mock-up of the wings—showed degrees of bank in a turn. Before the wings approached the 30-degree mark, I smoothly moved the stick back toward the center position so that just as my bank reached 30 degrees, the stick was centered to hold that 30-degree bank. If I then did nothing else to my flight controls after

I was in a 30-degree bank, I'd simply start "falling" slowly to the right, losing altitude and gaining airspeed. To stay level, with a constant airspeed, I had to do two very important things: (1) Pull back on the stick just the right amount to keep from losing altitude. What's the right amount? Only experience and "feel" can answer that. (2) Add just a bit of power, because by pulling back on the stick to keep altitude, I lost a bit of airspeed. Adding the right amount of power kept airspeed constant.

Unlike the T-41 and T-37, the T-38 needed no rudder during normal flight.

While I was flying in the back, Lieutenant Jackson, up front, besides watching for other aircraft, was also carefully watching my airspeed, altitude, and angle of bank on his instrument panel. Initially, the first few times I did this simple turn (and held the bank for a complete circle in the air), Lieutenant Jackson may have tolerated several degrees of bank over or under 30 degrees, the loss of several knots, and perhaps the loss or gain of several hundred feet in altitude. But as I practiced, the parameters shrank, and after several flights I was expected to stay *exactly* on airspeed, altitude, and bank—no deviation. None.

Why couldn't I just look at the altitude and airspeed on my flight instruments and hold the correct pressures? Because there was a slight lag in what the instruments told me. If I added power to gain a few knots, then the next thing I knew, I had overshot my airspeed. If I then pulled back on the throttle and waited for the right airspeed, I'd go through it and be on the slow side. Trying to "fly the instruments" resulted in continuous overcorrections. I learned to lead the instruments and to feel for needed adjustments. I remember Lieutenant Jackson saying, "Edgerton, you're about a half degree off your heading. The best way to get back is to *think* yourself to the correct heading. If you try to move the airplane, you'll probably overshoot."

After I'd mastered a 30-degree banked turn, I practiced 45-degree turns. A steeper bank makes it harder to hold your altitude and maintain an exact airspeed through the roll-in, during the turn, and then through the rollout. Next came turns with the aircraft in a 60-degree, or "steep-banked," turn. These were initially very difficult. The fact that I'd practiced them in the T-41 and T-37 didn't seem to be helping out.

Over the next few flights came 30-degree *descending* turns and 30-degree climbing turns. After those came 45-degree climbing and descending turns and then the same with the most difficult of all—60-degree turns.

Finally: "Okay, Edgerton, I want a forty-five-degree turn to a heading of one eight zero while you descend three hundred feet."

So I'm in this turn, watching my attitude indicator and feeling this 45-degree turn, trying to freeze it so I don't go over or under, and I'm glancing at my rate of descent indicator to be sure I don't overshoot that 300-foot descent, and I'm looking at my heading indicator, thinking about how much I need to lead my heading so that I smoothly roll out and find my wings level just as I reach a heading of 180 degrees—having descended *exactly* 300 feet. And way back there in the shade (in my mind) stands Lieutenant Jackson, hands on hips, ready to jump out into the sun, screaming his head off—at me. I'd heard rumors that if things got bad, Jackson turned into a screamer—in Captain Coleman's big league.

One day while in the backseat under the hood, Phil Ferguson, my classmate, was just under 10,200 feet up but misread the altimeter and thought he was at just under 200 feet above the ground, near the runway. He was coming in for a landing—he thought. He'd been 10,000 feet high for a while. It's understandable that an altimeter could be misread, though it takes a beginner or someone who's very confused. It's like looking at a clock that says 1:05 and believing it says 12:05.

Phil had started his final approach to landing from about 12,000 feet up (thinking he was at 2,000 feet) and Lieutenant Jackson hadn't said a word. Then Jackson asked, "How far are you from the ground, Ferguson?"

"Just under two hundred feet, sir." At about 200 feet, Jackson would normally take control of the airplane in order to land.

"Let's level her out."

Ferguson leveled the aircraft.

"How high are you now?"

"One hundred and eighty feet, sir."

"Could you get us back up to two hundred feet so we don't hit anything?"

"Yes, sir."

Ferguson, under the hood, is a little nervous at this point. There are radio towers and tall buildings in the area.

"Okay. We're skimming right above the trees, right?"

"Yes, sir."

My guess is that Jackson, up in the front seat, was tempted just to push the nose over and let the airplane go through where Ferguson thought the ground was, but he knew Ferguson might eject. "I have the aircraft. Pull back the hood, Lindbergh. Look around."

After a month or so of flying in the backseat under the hood, I then flew "contact" missions—missions from the front seat, still using instruments, but relying mostly on the world outside, while the instructor sat in the backseat.

"Okay, Edgerton," says Lieutenant Jackson. "I'll talk you through a loop. Let's line up with that road down there at three o'clock. Drop the nose. More. You're looking for five hundred knots. Okay, level out and give me a good four-g pull-up, straight up. Good. Keep the pressure in—keep pulling."

I'm tightening my stomach and leg muscles as the G suit squeezes tight.

Now the nose is pointed straight up.

"Watch your ADI [attitude indicator] for wings level. Good. Good. Let off a little pressure—that's too much buffet."

Then I'm falling over onto my back.

"Okay, good."

We're inverted.

"Two hundred knots. Keep the back pressure in. That's right. Look outside and keep those wings level. Back pressure, back pressure. Be smooth. Good."

Now we're pointed directly toward the ground. The airspeed is picking up dramatically.

"Ease off the back pressure. Whoa, not too much."

And now I'm coming back to where I started, lined up with the road, at 500 knots but a bit lower than the 15,000 feet we started with. I should be right on the button at the same altitude.

I was learning, step by step, to feel the aircraft as if it were a part of me, and aerobatics were preparing me for air-to-air combat with other aircraft—dogfighting—if I happened to end up in a jet fighter down the line. I couldn't imagine flying some big, slow airplane. But it could happen.

And of course I had to learn to land from the front seat, and flying the final turn to landing in the T-38 was difficult, more difficult than any procedure I'd encountered flying an airplane. Because there is nothing much to hold the aircraft up at slower speeds—the wings are relatively small—it seems to want to fall out of the sky while maneuvering at slow airspeeds. And because the wings are so far back on the fuselage, they are not much help to a pilot in sensing degree of bank in a turn.

In addition, I had to keep my power up while turning and descending in the aircraft and looking out at the runway, because letting a jet engine's power get too low means that acceleration, if you suddenly need it, will be slow. I was also, during this final turn, making a radio call, lowering the gear and flaps, and correcting for wind. It was a difficult series of maneuvers and actions in a short time. I'd be going relatively slow, and sinking, and applying back pressure on the stick to hold the turn. And in the mix was a final-turn aircraft buffet that occurred just prior to a stall. Stalling out in the final turn in the T-38 would mean no room below for recovery.

Traditionally, several pilots washed out of training while trying to learn to fly the final turn to landing in the T-38. I remember sitting in my room, working with the handle of a commode plunger up from the floor as if it were the stick in the aircraft and calling out my radio calls, looking back over my left shoulder, then looking back to where my airspeed indicator would be. That is the time I worked the hardest during pilot training—on that one maneuver: the T-38 final turn to landing. The cockpit was always the easiest part for me; the academics were more difficult.

It didn't help to know that in a class or two before mine, one of our current instructors, Lieutenant Smith, and a student had stalled out in the final turn and had both ejected—safely. I'd heard that Smith was the consummate screamer. I wondered if he'd been screaming before, during, and after the stall.

After touchdown, the most effective braking method was to pull back on the stick and raise the nose off the runway so that the entire belly of the aircraft served as a speed brake. That procedure seemed risky: if you raised the nose too early, you'd hop back into the air. But what wasn't risky about flying this airplane? Danger was always out there, just out of reach—you hoped. And for me and my buddies, that risk, plus our firm belief that we couldn't die before old age, made our flying lives an adventure.

Fingertip Formation

AFTER FLYING SEVERAL SOLO missions and a cross-country or two, I was eager for the final phase of training—flying in formation.

Put the fingers of your left hand together and look at the back of your hand. Pretend your four fingernails are airplanes. The lead aircraft, or number one, is the fingernail of your middle finger. Number two is your index-finger nail. Number three is your ring-finger nail, and four, your little-finger nail. That's how a "four-ship" often flies somewhere. The lead pilot, out front, is usually more experienced. He is looking around, navigating, making all decisions as if the flight of four were only one airplane. Every other pilot has his eyes glued to the aircraft next to and just in front of him.

On my first formation flight in the T-38, Lieutenant Jackson, in the backseat, didn't just suddenly fly the airplane into a fingertip position and then give me control. That would never work, because flying in formation is not unlike riding a bicycle—it's something you learn through trial and error, and at first, you're bad at it.

We were number two in a two-ship (the nails of your middle and index fingers) and Jackson was flying. (Much of our learning was in two-ship; only late in the program did we fly several flights of four-ship.) We moved into "route," or loose, formation; that is, we separated from the lead aircraft so that we could relax and glance inside our cockpit.

"You have the aircraft," said Jackson.

"I have the aircraft." I jiggled the stick to acknowledge that. (The stick has enough play in it so that at normal speeds, jiggling it doesn't cause the aircraft to jump around in the sky.) I found myself falling back a bit, so I added a little power; then when I was about even with the lead aircraft, I pulled my power back, but whoops, I was going right on past him. I'd added too much power, even though it was just a touch. And I'd somehow gotten too high, so I pushed the nose over just a bit and . . . whoops, I rapidly sank down below lead as I found myself *way out in front of him*. I was in *front* of *lead*. And down below him. I was looking up and back. So I corrected for that and found myself way back behind lead. The general problem was overcorrecting. I was all over the sky—below lead, above him, behind, ahead.

Gradually I learned to hold it steady out at a distance and then flew in a bit closer, and when I learned to steady it there, I finally moved into fingertip position. This didn't happen in one day. Several flights passed as I learned to make very tiny corrections in power and stick position—to anticipate and make small corrections before they were needed. For example, if I dropped back a few feet, I added power and then reduced it a bit even before the power kicked in. The two throttles in my left hand were inched up and back in tiny increments, first one, then the other, up and back, up and back, while I moved the stick left, right, back, forward, in very quick and tiny movements. When I became proficient, my airplane appeared to sit very still beside lead, while in fact I was making all those rapid, minute corrections with stick and throttle. At the same time, along with the other aircraft, I was moving through the air at several hundred miles an hour. Only if the flight was close to the ground did I get a sense of speed, and even when I was only twenty feet above the ground—in close formation—my eyes had to be glued to the lead aircraft, not the ground.

Pretend you're driving along on the interstate. You're in the right lane, behind but overtaking a car in the left lane. When the right rear taillight of the other car is lined up with the rearview mirror on your door, you slow to exactly the other car's speed. That car is now the leader and you are number two in a two-ship-formation flight. You must stay exactly that distance from the car—say, four feet out—and you must not move forward or backward; that is, your rearview mirror must stay *on* the taillight of the leader.

Airborne, you must also maintain the same altitude (up and down) as your leader. As he slows, speeds up, turns, climbs, dives, even flies upside down, you must maintain this relative position. Exactly. There is no ground below to hold you in place.

In a classic air-to-air duel—against another flight of four—the flight of four breaks up into two flights of two, and during the air duel each wingman moves out wide and behind his lead. The lead's job is to attack and shoot down an opponent. The wingman's job is to protect the lead, especially the area directly behind him—his "six o'-clock," where he cannot see well. In some situations, if number two is attacked, the lead serves in the protector role.

Number three and four might also work to protect one and two, and the four pilots could be talking to one another by radio if the situation demanded.

Now put the fingers of your *right* hand together and look at the back of your hand. A four-ship can also fly like this. Your index-finger nail would still be number two.

Let's go with the left hand. (The airplane represented by your little-finger nail would not be quite that far back—if your little finger is as short as mine—but rather it would be the same distance behind number three as numbers two and three are behind lead.)

One way of getting the flight together after takeoff is this: Lead takes off, slows down to a speed a bit slower than the normal climb-out speed, and turns into a shallow-banked right (or left) climbing turn. Number two takes off and cuts off lead, flying faster than lead on a course that will eventually intersect with lead (lead's speed was decided before takeoff, and everybody knows what it is). Number two gradually flies, from the right and behind lead, into the fingertip position, reducing power as he joins up so that when he's in position, he's flying at the same speed as lead.

As number two, I know that the join-up is going well if, as I approach the lead aircraft from far away, with the proper cutoff angle, the lead aircraft appears to stay at one position against my windshield. If he is slipping forward, I know that I will pass behind him, and if he is slipping backward, that I'll pass in front of him.

Properly done, joining on lead, as two, is extraordinarily beautiful and fun. There are no magic tricks for doing it right. It's a matter of correctly judging closure rate, relative speed, and position.

In the meantime, number three, having taken off after number two, also joins on lead (while keeping an eye on number two to avoid a collision). He flies just beneath both one and two and joins on lead's left wing, across from number two, who has already joined on lead's right wing. Throughout the join-up, the lead aircraft continues a shallow-banked turn—in our example, to the right. Shortly thereafter number four will join on number three's left wing.

A brilliant and amazing feat on the part of number three occurs when he—taking off *after* number two—joins on lead *before* number two gets there. This is done by playing angle, speed, and altitude just exactly right and cannot happen unless number two is lagging somehow—and number three is aggressive. (If you're number two, it's very embarrassing to have number three join on lead before you do.)

A formation of two or four aircraft may also taxi out to the runway in single file and then taxi onto the runway and line up to take off *all at the same time in fingertip for-*

mation. Head and hand signals — no radios — are often used in order to simulate combat conditions when enemy radio intercepts are possible. Everyone sits still, awaiting takeoff. The lead aircraft pilot, with a finger twirl, signals for engine run-up. All engines are run up to 100 percent for an engine check. Pilots are on the brakes, holding the aircraft still. Then two and three look at lead, and four looks at three. The lead looks around to verify that everyone is ready. He taps his helmet, leans his head back as if looking upward. Number three does the same while keeping an eye on the lead pilot. When lead drops his head, number three does the same, and simultaneously all pilots release brakes. The roll starts. Lead will use slightly less than full power so that the other aircraft will be able to maintain their proper positioning during the takeoff roll by jockeying their throttle settings. After liftoff, the lead pilot snaps his head back just before raising his landing gear, and three does the same, so that all can raise their gear together. The procedure is repeated for raising flaps. As they fly, the number two and three pilots watch the lead pilot, while number four watches number three.

After everyone is airborne, the lead pilot navigates, makes necessary radio calls to ground control, and looks around and makes decisions as if the flight of four were only one airplane. And while the lead aircraft pilot is doing all the thinking, what are the other pilots doing? Working their asses off, staying in formation. Let's say I'm number two. My eyes *stay* on the lead aircraft. I *never* let my eyes move away, even for a fraction of a second. Where am I looking? A star is painted on both sides of the fuselage (the main body) of the T-38. The star has a background of two stripes. The trailing edge of the T-38 wingtip has a red or green light on its tip (starboard green, port red). As number two (or three), flying beside and slightly behind and below number one, I will fly so that the wingtip light of number one appears to remain in the middle of the star on the side of his airplane. (Everybody except lead is doing the same thing.) When lead starts a left turn and his wing starts rising, my aircraft must rise so that the light stays in the star. An imaginary straight line runs from my eye, through the wingtip light, and to the middle of the star. This position will keep me neither too far forward nor too far back, neither too high nor too low. This fingertip formation enables us to fly through clouds while maintaining visual contact. Sometimes to see lead well in bad weather, I may have to "tuck it in" so that our wings overlap. In order to keep the proper distance away from his aircraft, I first learn the "right picture" of his exhaust ports — not too round, not too oval. Later I know by feel.

In fingertip formation we communicated by hand signals, as mentioned, and also by a very slight wiggling or bouncing of lead's aircraft. For example, if lead's tail end suddenly fishtailed a little bit (accomplished with rudder pedals), we knew to move into "route" formation, that is, loose formation. At that time we could quickly look inside our own aircraft to check fuel remaining, engine temperature, and so forth, and then look back at lead (though number four always looks at number three, who relays messages from lead when necessary).

When the pilot of the lead aircraft brought his thumb to his mouth in a drinking motion while the flight was in route formation, that meant "check your fuel." We then each signaled with upheld fingers how many hundreds of pounds of fuel we had left. The flight lead planned maneuvers according to the least amount of fuel among us.

When lead gently rocked his wings, we moved back into fingertip formation.

The lead pilot had to be extraordinarily smooth with the stick and throttles. An erratic movement—especially up or down—could set off a chain reaction.

If we were a *two*-ship formation—I was lead, and you were flying on my right wing—and I suddenly did a quick little dip of my left wing, that would be a signal for a "cross-under." You'd pull off a bit of power, drop back, add power, cross under just behind my exhaust ports (on the very tail end of the aircraft), and then add power again as you pulled up into position on my left wing—where number three would fly in a four-ship formation. The idea is to cross under quickly.

Another kind of formation—not fingertip—is called close trail. It can be flown in four-ship or two-ship formation. If I were your lead and I suddenly did a little porpoise with my nose (moving it up and down), you would know to slip back behind me and fly with the nose of your aircraft just behind and below my exhaust ports, and you would stay there no matter what I did. For example, I, the lead, might fly a loop or a barrel roll and you'd stay right there. And that would be hard work—for you. If, as number two, three, or four in close-trail formation, I could not feel the jet exhaust of the aircraft ahead skimming the top of my vertical stabilizer—the highest point on my aircraft—then I was flying too low. While flying close trail, or fingertip for that matter, a pilot learns the skills and limits of a wingman or leader the way I imagine competitive rowers must learn the skills and limits of their teammates.

Sometimes the formation missions were a bit scary. An instructor might have to take over an erratic aircraft. Someone might be closing too fast on a join-up and have to duck under the other aircraft at the last minute for a close miss.

In those four-ship missions late in the program, there would be three of us solo and an instructor flying lead. When we landed, we'd talk about the flight. I would almost be in a state of disbelief: How is it possible that we just did something so amazing and are here now together, talking about it?

Wings

AT THE END OF PILOT TRAINING, our individual flying grades and academic grades were averaged and we were ranked. The class was given a block of different types of airplanes (the combination differed from class to class) and each of us ranked our choices, with the top pilot getting his first choice and the bottom pilot getting the last remaining airplane.

I was nervous about my assignment—my flying grades were high, but my academic grades, only average. What if all the fighters were gone before my choice came up? What if our block of aircraft had no fighters? Sometimes that happened.

Practically everybody wanted a fighter, and nobody wanted a bomber, especially the B-52. Flying the B-52, we were told, was boring—hours of doing nothing at a very high altitude out of range of surface-to-air missiles (SAMs) and then a few seconds of pressing a button to release bombs, then more hours of nothing.

Bombers and cargo planes were flown with yokes instead of sticks, and with throttles on the right. A fighter had a stick up from the floor and throttles on the left—like the T-37 and the T-38. The presence of a stick and the placement of the throttles were associated with speed, agility, and adventure. Both the T-37 and the T-38, with a few modifications, had been made into fighters—the A-37 and the F-5.

The Air Force philosophy in my day was to teach each of us to fly a fighter so that we could quickly adapt to any aircraft in the Air Force. The Navy split their pilots into fighter and cargo categories early in their pilot training, as the Air Force does now.

A few of our student pilots—Dickson, Bynum, and Williams—wanted to fly a big cargo plane, a C-130 or a C-135. (*F* is for *fighter, B* for *bomber, C* for *cargo, T* for *trainer,* and *OV* for *observation.*)

The F-104 I had seen on TV in "the film" when I was a boy was rarely assigned anymore. I wanted a single-seat fighter—an F-100, 101, 102, or 105—and if not one of those, then the relatively new, very hot, dual-seat F-4.

But what about those average academic grades? I was not at the top of the class. Had I come this far to end up in a damn bomber or cargo plane—something that wouldn't fly upside down and faster than the speed of sound?

The list came down, and slots for my squadron included four F-105s, four F-100s, and, luckily, eleven F-4s. I got an F-4. Nineteen of us got fighters and twenty-three of us got a mix of nonfighter aircraft.

THE F-4 WAS THE FASTEST and most powerful fighter in the world, and my six-month training course in how to fly it would be at Homestead Air Force Base, just south of Miami, Florida. We'd learn not only the specifics of flying the airplane, not greatly different from flying the T-38, but also its missions: air-to-air combat, air-to-ground, and nuclear. But first came a three-week survival training course at Fairchild Air Force Base in Washington State.

I remember writing home, and saying aloud proudly to anyone interested—or not: "My assignment will be F-4 backseat to Miami."

On our last day in Laredo, family members came to the ceremony for the awarding of wings. My mother flew on her first commercial flight, as I had a year earlier—to Laredo. There she pinned my silver wings onto my dress blues during the graduation ceremony.

"My, my," she said. "That little trip to the airport all those years ago—leading up to this. My, my."

"This is just the beginning," I said.

We never spoke of war.

PART 3

(1968–70)

FLYING JET FIGHTERS

Survival Training

WHAT DO YOU DO after bailing out of an aircraft behind enemy lines or over a wilderness area? I was sent to Fairchild Air Force Base in Washington State to find out. After Fairchild, I'd start my F-4 training at an eight-week radar-operation course at Davis-Monthan Air Force Base in Tucson, Arizona (the F-4 radar was operated from the rear seat, and all training at Davis-Monthan would be in a flight simulator), and then I'd be back to Florida for six months of flying the F-4.

During our survival training, I and a new set of comrades—fighter-pilots-to-be as well as air crews of big airplanes—would take two weeks of academic classes and physical training in preparation for six days in the wild.

Within a few days of arriving at Fairchild, I met Buddy Harmon, another F-4 backseater. Buddy, from Alabama, was short and round faced and spoke with a southern twang I'd heard little of—except from my own mouth—in the past year.

During those first two weeks we learned, among other skills, how to get out of our parachute harnesses on the ground in high wind. We were taken in buses to a flat area where a very large wind fan stood ready and waiting. I hooked myself into a parachute harness and lay down on the ground; then the parachute was held up to catch the wind from the fan, the fan was turned on, and I fumbled with my harness releases as I was dragged along, learning how to release myself quickly so as not to be dragged by wind.

We were fed cooked dog, horse, and snake, just to show us that it wasn't so bad. We had lectures, demonstrations, and practice about how to, among other skills, choke someone with a belt or a short piano wire with handles and how to hold, aim, and fire the .38 pistol, a weapon we'd carry in our survival vests on combat missions. We took judo classes. My mind's eye could dimly see an enemy soldier. I felt better knowing how to use these weapons, but I suspected that I'd never need them, and I think most of us felt that way.

"Where in hell we gonna get a piano wire?" asked Buddy.

I hadn't thought about it. "From a piano?"

And then, after a couple of weeks of running everywhere on base (we were not allowed to walk outdoors), we were taken on buses to a training camp in the Washington wilderness, where we were shown how to use our ponchos to build a camouflaged shelter beneath leaves and dirt, how to build a makeshift lean-to, how to trap animals, how to travel quietly and unseen.

On the day before we'd be turned loose in pairs—out

of base camp and into the wilderness with maps and compass and forty pounds of equipment each on our backs to be chased by "enemy" troops with dogs—the fourteen in my group were given a live rabbit. After being shown how to kill it, skin it, gut it, and cook it, we did all that. Then each of us ate about one-fourteenth of a tender, freshly grilled rabbit. That's the last "real" food we'd have for several days. Packed into our backpacks for our three-day trek in the mountains were two cereal bars and two bars of something called pemmican, a kind of beef jerky.

Sergeant Webber was my partner in the wilderness. He would eventually be a crew member on a cargo plane. Together, he and I were to navigate through the cold Washington wilderness for two days, sleeping under our two ponchos (snapped together into a small tent) and running from "Communist soldiers" manning dogs on leashes—out to get us. Our job was to stay ahead of them, navigating with our compasses and maps through manned checkpoints in the woods to a final staging area. If we were caught and released, or if we were late to a checkpoint or missed one, a card we carried would be punched. Three punches and we'd have to repeat our last three days of the wilderness program. A few days before we arrived, a pilot, taken to the hospital because of exposure and exhaustion, had died from pneumonia.

The Washington mountains in our area were not high; they were climbable, steep hills. We wore regular, government-issue combat boots. Had snow been forecast, we would have been issued snow boots—inflatable rubber boots, designed to keep our feet warm and dry.

Unforecast snow fell our first night out, blanketing everything. We had many fallen logs to cross and we were carrying those forty-pound backpacks. I remember how difficult it was to stand after slipping to the ground, and near the end of our trek, when we'd take a break to rest, I could imagine curling up and going to sleep, or just lying still, not moving.

On the first night, I left my wet gloves outside the tent flap. The next morning they were frozen.

"Webber, have we got time to build a little fire and thaw these things out?"

"I think I hear the dogs . . . hear that?"

After the two days and a night running from the enemy and navigating through the wilderness, we all, about thirty of us, converged. But for the last hundred yards or so before being automatically captured, we had to crawl on our stomachs through a large field. If one of us hit a trip wire, a flare ignited, and the offender's card was punched.

After capture, we were herded into a fenced-in compound commanded by "Communist soldiers" wearing uniforms and small-billed hats with red stars on the front. Our job was to organize for escape. Within the first few hours we were gathered into small groups and lectured on the glory of Communism and the evil of capitalism. I argued with the lecturers. An enemy officer pulled me aside and said, "Academic situation." This was code for "We are no longer playing war. I have something important to tell you." He told me I should not argue. To do so would guarantee my being picked for interrogation. My argumentativeness would be seen as a sign of weakness, not strength.

We were put into wooden boxes, each about the size of a small telephone booth—just under six feet tall by about three feet square. We had to stand (but I couldn't stand straight, being six feet two) for twelve hours, overnight. We were given water but no food. At some point during the stay in the large box, we were each taken out and put into a box just big enough to hold someone wedged in on hands and knees. This was for, as I recall, a few hours. Then came interrogation. We'd all been given secret information about our units, and our job was not to squeal. After the interrogation—two guys holding sticks and hollering—one of the guys called an academic situation and told me I'd done fine.

I remember, while in the big box and awaiting my time in the little box, hearing a voice nearby that I'd never heard, a southern, nasal, Gomer Pyle twang: "I ain't getting in that box. I don't care what you say. I ain't getting in that box. I don't care what you do. You can punch my card a thousand times. I ain't getting in that box. You can kill me, but I ain't . . ."

After three days of no food except for the cereal, the pemmican bars, and one-fourteenth of a rabbit, we were all marched to a gathering place by a road, where a mush of some sort was being cooked in large metal trash cans over fires. We were allowed one ladle each, and I remember how hot it was, how it burned my tongue, how it tasted with no salt. We were then bused back to Fairchild Air Force Base.

We rode along, listless, but then someone saw a sign advertising hamburgers. "Hamburger," he said. "Milk," said another. "Mashed potatoes." "Biscuits." "Apple pie."

I remember standing before a mirror after a shower in my quarters. I could see the outlines of my ribs. My lips were split from being chapped. My palms were covered with small cuts because after my gloves froze and I could no longer wear them, I held on to branches of small fir trees while slipping and sliding down hillsides, and sometimes a branch would cut my hand or finger.

And my feet: One night, during snowfall, I put my wet boots too close to our campfire to dry out. The soles bubbled up, the boots shrank, and in order to get them on the next morning, I had to cut slits in them. They left blisters.

I headed for the officer's club dining room. (Several days later I'd find out that I had lost twenty pounds during my six weeks.)

In the dining room, several of us were seated at a table. In front of me sat a crisp green salad—on a clean white tablecloth. I said to the others, "That's a crisp green salad. It's on a clean white tablecloth."

I ordered a steak, but my stomach had shrunk so much I couldn't finish it.

Buddy, from Alabama, was at my table. "Bet you can't eat dessert," he said.

"You're right," I said.

"Pussy."

I ordered apple pie and ice cream and ate it all.

Next day, we were free to leave. Buddy and I started for Davis-Monthan Air Force Base in Tucson, Arizona, in his car. We'd have our eight-week radar-training course there before moving on to our F-4 training at Homestead.

"One thing I'll never do as long as I live is miss another meal," I said as we drove south through Washington State.

"Me too. For sure."

Down through Oregon and California we each ordered a steak or a hamburger at every meal. I ate apple pie and ice cream whenever it was on the menu.

But somehow we didn't plan well. On the second or third day of our trip, crossing the Nevada desert, we realized that (1) it was lunchtime, and (2) we had only one thin dime between us. We bought a Hershey's chocolate bar with almonds from a service station, split it, and ate it slowly and silently as we looked out across the desert.

The F-4

AFTER EIGHT WEEKS IN TUCSON, I was shipped to Miami, where I bought a motorcycle and found an apartment with a new friend, another F-4 backseater, Nick Lawrence.

There were about forty of us in all in the new training class—twenty front-seaters and twenty backseaters, including two buddies from Laredo pilot training, Bill Steele and Jerry Daughtry. The front-seat trainees were old-timers from other aircraft or former F-4 backseaters. Those of us fresh out of pilot training were backseaters.

Either the front-seater (the "aircraft commander") or the backseater (the "pilot") did the flying with his own set of controls. The backseater, besides flying, operated the navigation equipment as well as the radar system that tracked enemy aircraft and mapped the ground.

At Homestead, first morning of training, we all met in a large classroom. I was introduced to Colonel John Poole, the front-seater I'd be training with after instructors taught each of us the fundamentals of flying the F-4. He was new to the F-4 too. He'd been on nonflying status for three years, stationed at the Pentagon. He was a short, balding, feisty forty-eight-year-old, and from my perch at age twenty-four, he seemed ancient. I quickly learned, however, that Colonel Poole was an excellent pilot, just a bit rusty. He'd flown a P-38 (a hot fighter) in World War II. On a bombing pass, ground fire through the cockpit had taken off a piece of the throttle and part of his left index finger.

After we'd flown together a few times, Colonel Poole started calling me Killer. Nick and I invited him over to our apartment for dinner several times, and I remember a late afternoon walk with the old colonel. He talked to me about his marriage, about how he and his wife had changed over the years. I remember few specifics from the conversation, but I do remember that I felt from him a kind of fatherly friendship.

Together we students flew in flights of four with an instructor flying the front seat of the lead aircraft. We flew gunnery-range missions, dropping practice bombs (they are a little bigger than a shoe box and leave a smoke trace on impact), shooting practice rockets (they're small and self-propelled and leave a smoke trace also) and the twenty-millimeter gun in the nose of the aircraft. It shot a hundred real bullets (no practice rounds) per *second,* and the noise it made, rather than rat-tat-tat, was like a deep-throated groan. A blast much longer than two seconds would melt the gun barrel (the kind of thing I relished telling my buddies back home).

Normally our missions lasted about an hour and a half and were flown in two-ship or four-ship formation. That time was extended if we carried an external centerline fuel tank beneath the belly of the aircraft. Some missions required staying in the air even longer, so we had to learn air-to-air refueling techniques. Both pilots were required to be proficient.

Air-to-air refueling occurs in the smooth air of high altitudes. A flight of four F-4s approaches a C-135 tanker and flies in formation several hundred yards out to the side and behind it. The fighters, one at a time, leave the F-4 formation and fly to a position just below and to the rear of the C-135 and remain in a kind of close-trail formation while being refueled.

I once filmed a refueling with my Super-8 camera. The camera pointed up and forward through the canopy (Colonel Poole was flying), and in my movie the underbelly of the C-135 fills the screen. And there's the face of the boom operator looking through his little window. The boom (a long pole-hose) is being extended toward us. It reaches just above our heads, swaying slightly, aimed at the receptacle in the top of the aircraft, just behind my head. We sense it click into place after a moment and then sit there taking on fuel while flying in formation. We appear to be sitting still beneath the tanker, but in fact we and the tanker are flying at about three hundred knots. The constantly increasing weight of our aircraft, caused by the onloading of fuel, means tiny adjustments in trim and power setting are required for us to stay in position.

• • •

WE ALSO FLEW MISSIONS in which a pair of air-craft were matched against another pair in air-to-air combat. Two aircraft would take off and fly to a general area. The other two aircraft would take off, and at a certain time, with neither flight of two knowing exactly where the other was, the battle would begin—two against two. Each flight of two would try to find the other on radar, which could "see" up to fifty miles or so and could simulate kills with a pretend radar-guided missile inside about thirteen miles. The backseater's job was to find the other aircraft on his radar screen, then "lock on" with a radar beam. (This is what we backseaters learned to do at Davis-Monthan Air Force Base in Arizona after survival training.) The aircraft would then be positioned for the mock shooting of a radar missile and a kill, verified by a call of "Fox One" on the radio from the aircraft doing the simulated shooting. After that, when one flight saw the other, there'd be a dogfight in which each flight tried to simulate shooting down the other, first with heat-seeking missiles (for distances from three thousand to nine thousand feet) and then with the twenty-millimeter canon in the nose of the aircraft for shooting inside about one thousand feet.

A kill with a heat-seeking missile was verified by the victor calling, "Fox Two."

The most prized call (from our aircraft) during a dogfight was "Fox Three," for this meant that in the rough-and-tumble of fighting in the air, you had gotten on the tail of the enemy aircraft and stayed close enough, and at the right angle, long enough to shoot him down with your guns. Many fights ended in a stalemate, with two aircraft flying across from each other in a very tight circle (called a lufbery), slowly losing altitude. If one broke away, the other would be on his tail. At five thousand feet up we were required to break it off, and that last part of the battle would be declared a draw.

Prior to the air-to-air combat training, Colonel Poole and I were embarrassed when leading a flight home one night. From the backseat I was not paying as much attention to the details of our flight as I should have been. I trusted the colonel. But he led our flight of four F-4s into the VFR traffic pattern from the wrong direction. Had the flight continued, all aircraft would have landed into oncoming traffic. The consequences could have included a collision. This is why instructors went along on training missions. The instructor in one of the aircraft on this flight caught the mistake and ordered the flight of four to break up and reenter traffic, each aircraft on its own. It was terribly embarrassing—for anybody, but especially for this sassy colonel, who liked to ask hard questions during academic lectures. And for his backseater. "Killer," indeed.

So, late in the program, when the time came for air-to-air combat, we had something to prove. One flight stands out in memory, along with a handful of others, from my Air Force career: our last scheduled air-to-air combat mission in F-4 training.

We briefed. Four trainees would be in the front seats of the two flights of two. Three trainees and an instructor would be in the backseats.

By this time, Colonel Poole and I were working well together. During dogfights when our opponent was behind us and I could see him but the colonel couldn't, I was able to give a running commentary about exactly where the other guy was and what he was doing. And the colonel's World War II air-to-air training was coming in handy.

I'd say, "He's at five o'clock, low at five hundred yards, climbing, and gaining."

The colonel then might crank in a six- or seven-g right turn.

"Now he's at three."

"I have him, I have him," the colonel would say. "If I can . . . if I can just . . ."

"He's overshooting! Reverse [abruptly change direction of turn]!"

"There—we've got him." And we'd suddenly be on our opponent's tail.

This last flight was a kind of world series. Bets were placed.

Three times we locked horns with another aircraft—close-in. Fox 3 battles were usually standoffs. Occasionally someone would win one. Rarely, two. Three times on this particular mission we scored a Fox 3.

"I can't believe it," I said.

"Well, I can. We showed 'em, Killer."

The two flights of two were joining up to head home. The battles were over. Number two joined on lead. Number three joined on lead. We were number four. I was flying. As we moved in to join up, the colonel said, "I have the aircraft." But rather than join up, he flew away from and out in front of the other three aircraft. Do you remember how after an aircraft won an air victory in those old air-battle war films, it celebrated with a "victory roll," a slow aileron roll? That's what Colonel Poole did. We were showing off, celebrating, and we could almost feel the other pilots gritting their teeth.

After landing, a van, as usual, came around to pick up the pilots. Colonel Poole and I were walking back to the flight building. The other six pilots were in the van when it stopped for us. The colonel said to me as it pulled up and stopped, "Don't get in." He stuck his head in and said to the driver, "We're walking in. We're too good to ride with these goof-offs."

There was no response. The van pulled away.

Before finishing at Homestead, we took a water-survival course, similar to our training at Fairchild AFB in Washington State but without the hardship. Water survival was great fun. We got to play in the water for six days. Hanging from lanyards, we rode long, slanted wires down into water to simulate hitting the water in a parachute. We were each dragged in a parachute harness behind a boat, simulating being dragged by wind across the water. While being dragged along, we had to learn to flip onto our backs, spread our legs to stay on our backs, and release the parachute harness. We each strapped into a cockpitlike device that was suddenly submerged in a swimming pool. We released ourselves from the harness, opened the canopy, and escaped.

We parasailed across Biscayne Bay behind a speedboat several hundred feet below. An instructor on the boat called, "Release!" through a megaphone.

I detached myself from the line that was pulling me,

and then as I floated down, hanging in the parasail parachute, I reached to the package on my butt and released a self-inflating raft and a survival kit. They dangled below me as I descended. I inflated the float devices under my arms — life preservers — and as I descended, the instructor called, "Turn left," "Turn right," and "Prepare to land." I followed his instructions, turning left by pulling on the left riser and right by pulling on the right one. The parasail type of chute did not drop straight down but rather at a gliding angle, so I determined my direction of drift and turned myself in to the wind to minimize drift on impact.

I hit the water, then released the parachute from my harness and pulled it in. (Had the parachute landed on my head, I would have found any single cord embedded in the silk and followed it until it reached the border of the parachute so that I could peep out, gather up the chute, and store it.) I pulled the life raft to me, climbed in, pulled in my survival kit (attached to the life raft), opened it, and retrieved and put on my sun hat.

Also in the survival kit were packets of shark repellent — a black inky liquid. The rumor was that its purpose was to banish the pilot's anxiety, but not sharks.

I converted seawater to drinking water with a purification tablet. I found suntan lotion in the survival kit and applied it to exposed skin. I thought about home, about the war, about friends, about what I was going to do that night.

Then I sat in the raft for several hours, there in Biscayne Bay, not far from Miami, Florida, looking to the horizon, trying to spot any of the other guys who were out there with me, imagining that if this adventure were real, I'd be picked up and flown to waiting reporters as a hero.

I heard the drone of the rescue helicopter. I'd been taught the routine: wait for the helicopter to hover nearby and drop the rescue device, which was attached by a metal line, and then after the device hit the water and released static electricity, climb out of my raft, float (with my underarm floats) over to the device, fold down one of the three seats, climb onto it, hold on, and give a thumbs-up to be pulled up into the helicopter and flown back to the Air Force base.

While at Homestead, we were allowed to request our next assignments—where we wanted to go to fly the F-4: Vietnam, Japan, or the States. This was late summer 1968. Pilots were being shot down regularly over North Vietnam, South Vietnam, and Laos. I was in no special hurry to go to war. I asked for Japan as my first choice, then the States, and then Southeast Asia (known in Air Force literature as SEA). It was common knowledge that if our first assignment wasn't SEA, then the second one would be.

But I didn't bother to think that far ahead.

I got my first preference and was on the way to Yokota Air Base, Japan.

First Assignment: Japan and Korea

I ARRIVED AT YOKOTA in the fall of 1968. From the hallway window just outside my door in BOQ 16 (bachelor officers' quarters) at Yokota Air Base I could see Mount Fuji on clear days. Though the roar of departing jets sometimes broke the tranquillity of the scene, that didn't bother me at the time. An F-4 fighter wing—two squadrons, about forty pilots in each—was stationed on base. My squadron was the Thirty-fifth TFS (tactical fighter squadron). The other was the Eightieth.

Our mission in Japan worked like this: One squadron would leave Yokota and spend five weeks at Osan Air Base in South Korea. The other squadron would relieve that one, and the first would return to Yokota. The second squadron would spend five weeks in Osan and then return, and both squadrons would be on base at Yokota together for five weeks while an F-4 squadron from elsewhere served in Korea.

A pilot in the Eightieth TFS, Jim Butts, had been in my

training class at Laredo, though not in my squadron, so I didn't know him well. We would become roommates for my eighteen months in Japan—and close friends to this day. Since he was in the other fighter squadron on base, he and I would be rooming together in the BOQ in Yokota for five weeks, and then I'd be gone to Korea for five weeks, and when I got back, he'd be gone for five weeks.

Soon after arriving in Japan, before I had had an opportunity to fly any training missions, I was shipped to Korea. During our five-week tours in Korea, for several four-day stretches at a time, I'd be among a group of eight pilots living in the "alert shack," a large two-story brick building with living quarters upstairs, and eating and lounging facilities downstairs. The alert shack was near the alert hangars, where our four aircraft were waiting, each with a nuclear bomb strapped underneath. South Korea is close to Russia, and we were prepared to strike Russian military complexes.

When not sitting alert in Korea, we'd fly normal training missions, like those we'd flown in Florida. Our mission, besides nuclear alert, was to stay combat ready for either conventional (nonnuclear) air-to-air or air-to-ground combat.

I didn't sit alert right away, and my first mission was flown with Captain Cam Knight, a spark plug from South Carolina. He and I would play many games of Ping-Pong in the months to come. I rarely won.

The Korean landscape we flew over looked rich and green. Villages of thatched-roof huts dotted the countryside.

As our flight of four was coming in to land after an air-intercept mission (we were the lead in a flight of four), Captain Knight, flying the aircraft, said to me, "We need to do a bubble check."

"What's a bubble check, sir?"

"Stand by."

As we neared the base, Captain Knight called the tower and asked permission for a bubble check. Permission was granted.

Normally a flight of four would fly directly above the runway in the direction of landing at fifteen hundred feet up and at an airspeed of 300 knots. The flight of four would fly in right-echelon formation (like the fingernails on your right hand if your index finger were longer than your middle finger, with the lead aircraft being the index-finger nail) to a point about halfway down the runway, and then the lead would suddenly break left (make a sharp, level, 180-degree left turn) while the other fighters kept straight ahead, wings level. After five seconds, number two would break left, and so on, until the four aircraft were in a straight line, one behind the other, for landing—each would land after making a final 180-degree descending turn to the runway. But as we neared the base, we were headed down the runway not at fifteen hundred feet, not at 300 knots. We were at fifty feet and 450 knots. And we were not in echelon formation; we were in finger-tip formation. What was going on?

Our flight of four, in effect, buzzed the base, streaking down the runway as if we were the Thunderbirds (the Air Force aerobatic team, which flies in air shows).

Nothing was said and we reentered the normal pattern and landed without incident. On the ground I asked another backseater what the hell *bubble check* meant.

"Oh, in the old days a pilot would see if his compass was working by flying down a runway with a known heading. That's all. Now it's just a chance to show off."

Later that same day an order came down from headquarters: No more bubble checks. I'd flown on the very last official bubble check at Osan Air Base, Korea. Such a maneuver would never have been made on a base in the States or in Japan, but flight restrictions in Korea were more relaxed than in other places I had flown and would fly, until Southeast Asia.

As mentioned earlier, one of the main reasons we went to Korea was to stand by for—and then if called, be a part of—nuclear war. The Air Force F-4 was the first fighter-bomber (as opposed to a bomber) used as a platform (military jargon) for dropping not only conventional bombs, but also nuclear bombs. The presence of two pilots rather than only one created a security umbrella: a single person could not take off with and then drop a nuclear bomb. Big bombers with large crews had this check in place.

THERE WAS SOME DELAY in finding a regular front-seater for me, so I flew with a number of other pilots. I was granted Christmas leave (1968), and just before departing Japan, I was assigned to Captain Mike Tressler's backseat. Tressler was a flamboyant sort—tall, blond hair. When sitting alert, he wore two pearl-handled revolvers. I had flown with him a couple of times before I left for the

States, never taking the opportunity to get the story be-hind the revolvers. Another backseater, new to the squadron, and whom I hadn't met, was assigned to Tressler's back-seat temporarily.

At home I received a phone call from Japan. Captain Tressler and his temporary backseater, on a routine night mission in Japan, after a go-around from a missed ap-proach, had flown into a low hill and had both been killed. I was stunned. I wondered who was flying. I remembered the time Colonel Poole had entered traffic from the wrong direction, when I might as well have been asleep in the backseat. I wondered if the backseater could have saved his and Mike's lives.

Had I not been home on leave, I might have been dead.

I didn't tell my parents what the call was about. I didn't want to think about dying in an airplane, and there was nothing I could do about what had just happened. It was Christmas in North Carolina.

No one would dare brief an illegal maneuver, and no maneuver was supposed to be flown that was not briefed (discussed by all the pilots) before the flight. This rule was generally followed, with one exception. The ex-ception was especially prevalent in Korea. If a flight of four happened to be within visual sight of another flight of four, and no officer above captain or perhaps major was in either flight, then the chances of a free-for-all dog-fight—one of our four-ships against the other—were high. Very soon after arriving in Korea, I found myself involved in one. These dogfights were legitimate when the mission called for them and they were briefed, but impromptu dogfights were illegal. No one involved ever told, and there was the feeling that any commander would have turned a blind eye—unless an accident happened.

The chance of an accident during these events was not low. Each flight of four in a dogfight would have turned their flight's radios to a "discrete frequency," meaning that only that flight was talking on and listening to that frequency, and eight identical F-4s would be all over the sky, one group of four trying to score Fox 3s on the other four. Each flight would have split into two flights of two with a lead and a wingman. While the radio communication between aircraft in a flight was relatively heavy during these dogfights, the communication between front seat and backseat in an individual F-4 was almost constant, as with Colonel Poole and me back in F-4 training. The air duel was a chess game, and the object was to end up at your opponent's six o'clock position (directly behind him), situated so that a burst of your gunfire would shoot him down. The long-distance missile shoot-down business didn't count in these games. My guess is that many of us had old air-to-air combat war-movie scenes unreeling in our heads.

An aircraft closing from behind ours usually meant that the front-seater of my aircraft was about to pull the aircraft into a tight six-g (or greater) turn. This meant I was about to gray out or black out for a second or two. As soon as I was able, I was all talk again. "I don't have him, I don't have him. There he is. He's at five o'clock! He's overshooting. He's overshooting . . . now! Reverse!" And if we were very lucky, we could snap to the right—out of our hard left turn—pull, hit afterburner, be all over his ass, and say into the radio on a frequency that the other aircraft could hear: "Fox Three."

If someone behind us called, "Fox Three," while we were in a sharp turn and we could not see the belly of his aircraft, then he did *not* have the necessary lead through his sights to shoot us down, and on landing we could tell him that, nullifying the kill.

Most of the illegal dogfights were between F-4s, between those of us who knew one another. The stakes shot to the sky, however, when we came across a flight of F-101s, also based at Osan. The F-101s belonged to an air-defense group and were painted gray instead of camouflage. They were single-seat, single-engine fighters, designed strictly for air-to-air combat. Rarely did their pilots and ours socialize. They lost some status because our aircraft was more powerful and sophisticated than theirs. We lost some status because two of us flew the F-4, while only one pilot flew the F-101; we also lost status because we had an extra engine in case one failed. They had no backup. Whenever the opportunity arose in the air, we'd jump them, or they'd jump us. The rivalry was intense.

That there were no air-to-air collisions during any of these unauthorized dogfights (or during the authorized ones, which were a part of training) seems remarkable. I was once in a one-on-one dogfight with another F-4 and we lost sight of each other. A few minutes passed. I was craning around in my seat, looking everywhere, as was the front-seater. Suddenly I saw a speck directly in front of us. It was getting larger.

"I think . . . I think . . . is that . . . that's them! Watch—"

We were each going over four hundred miles an hour and closing fast—head-on. My front-seater swerved our aircraft. We learned later that they never saw us.

Back in Japan, our flying was more restrained. Additionally, we flew less in Japan than in Korea, but in Japan, on base, there was much more partying than in Korea. I quickly acclimated. There was always a big party in Japan just before the squadron left for Korea, and another on return.

My roommate, Jim Butts, and I ribbed each other fairly constantly. Jim kidded me about my furniture. I used a cardboard box for a bedside table in my room. He kidded me about my clothes. I had only two pairs of khakis. He was a bit more stylish. We each have tales about the other, and when I last saw him in 2004, we were still laughing at the same old stories.

Together, Jim and I bought a black sedan, a Cedric, with the steering wheel on the right. It was heavy, like a tank, and we double-dated in it, routinely confused when driving off base—on the left side of the road.

On one occasion I hid my portable cassette tape recorder—recording—under the front seat while we were out on the town.

"Watch it!" "Whoa, there." "Don't—what are you *doing?!*"

FOUR OF US put together an informal blues band. Sam Shelton, a backseater from my squadron, played harmonica; I played piano; Jerry Finnegan, a dentist, played guitar; and Gary Amstead, a navigator, played tenor saxophone. Often just Sam and I played in the officer's club bar, in Japan as well as in Korea. He kept a pair of drum brushes and a harmonica in a flight suit pocket below his knee, and somewhere in the officer's club at Yokota and Osan he stored a round cardboard cutout that served as a drum surface. He'd find an aluminum lampshade for a cymbal. We played Ramsey Lewis's "The In Crowd," Ray Charles's "What'd I Say," and any number of Mose Allison and Mercy Dee Walton tunes. After a few songs, Sam would lay aside his drum brushes and play harmonica. He introduced me to the harmonica style of bluesman Sonny Terry, and when I later heard a Sonny Terry album for the first time, it sounded to me as if Sonny Terry had learned from my buddy Shelton rather than the other way around.

One apartment or another in the BOQ in Japan housed a big party several times a month. At the end of the officer's club Go-Go Night on Saturday nights or Mexican Food Night in the dining room on Wednesday nights, you might hear over the intercom: "Party in room seven" (or one or fourteen).

An international hotel that housed flight attendants from major U.S. airlines during layovers was located five minutes from the base. The officer's club was a convenient outing for them, and many ended up at our parties.

There was a large, empty grass lot just across from the BOQ. On weekends in spring and summer, in the late afternoon, we'd have coed touch-football games there that sometimes lasted until after dark. A blanket in the end zone nearest the BOQ held ice, drinks, and food, and long breaks in the games for rest and refreshments weren't unusual.

Sometimes pilots would attempt "carrier landings" in the officer's club. Several large tables would be cleaned off and placed end-to-end. Beer was poured on their surfaces to reduce friction. A pilot backed away from the table as far as possible—sometimes into an adjoining room—took a running start, and dove headfirst onto the tables, arms pinned to his side (this was mandatory) to see how far he could slide before coming to a stop. Injuries were not uncommon. Especially if you were going fast enough to continue off the far side of the carrier.

Normally our wing and squadron commanders overlooked the antics of younger pilots, especially those of us in BOQ 16. But on one occasion just after a new base commander had arrived, we threw an unusually active party during which our building was damaged. Seven or eight of us were ordered to headquarters for questioning. The commander, accompanied by a mystery guest, sat with us around a table in a lush meeting room.

"Who lives in room sixteen?" he asked.

We looked at one another. Butch Henderson and Lynn Snow were in Korea for their five-week tour.

"They're in Korea," someone said.

"Okay, here's the deal," said the commander. "This man sitting beside me is a military attorney. He handles my legal matters, and if this kind of destruction of property happens again, the ones responsible will be off this base like shit through a tin horn."

We toned down. Interesting turn of phrase. I'd never heard it before—and haven't since.

An Air Force pilot automatically accrued the informal status of the aircraft he flew. While the status of any particular aircraft can be argued about endlessly, a general ranking went something like this: fighter pilots were at the top of the heap, along with pilots of the A-1E, an old single-engine tail dragger—a World War II fighter. The A-1E could sustain hits from ground fire, was slow enough to have a low-radius turn, and could make many gunnery passes in a short time, and it was thus used regularly in efforts to rescue downed pilots in Southeast Asia. The tier below fighter pilots included pilots of Gooney Birds—the old C-47s from World War II, a big tail dragger with twin engines (like the airplane you see at the end of *Casablanca*). One of the pilots in my Laredo pilot-training class who finished high enough to choose a fighter, chose a Gooney Bird instead. It was a sentimental favorite. There was buzz about a new airplane designed for the war in Vietnam, the OV-10. It was a small, powerful turboprop aircraft with a cockpit designed like a fighter jet's. It was used for reconnaissance and directing air strikes, and in a pinch it could transport up to six soldiers in a cargo bay.

In the next echelon were big cargo planes, and at the top of that batch was the C-130, designed to make low passes over jungle strips and drop cargo from the rear of the fuselage.

At the bottom of all mental lists that I ever knew about was the B-52, mentioned earlier.

Beneath all pilots (in the eyes of the pilots) were navigators, regardless of the aircraft they navigated. Most pilots who washed out of pilot training went to navigator-training school, and there was no shortage of navigator jokes. Navigators, on the other hand, considered themselves the brains of any flying mission. They left the steering to the dummy called the pilot, and they had their jokes too.

Backseat F-4 pilots held a unique position. Most were lieutenants just out of pilot training who'd been promised a quick upgrade to the front seat. But about the time I came along, the promise of an upgrade to front seat after six months became a joke. In most cases it didn't happen, and then by the time it did, an extra two-year commitment (beyond the basic five years) came with it.

Because backseaters often flew the aircraft (I flew most of the formation flying during my flights), we were afforded fighter-pilot status, but among F-4 front-seat pilots we were merely GIBs—the guy in back. The backseater's standing joke was, "Remember that GIB spelled backwards is BIG."

Backseat was a worthwhile position for a young fighter pilot. I navigated, controlled the radar, and was able to learn from the front-seater. Though I normally flew with the same front-seater, I occasionally flew with someone new, giving me the opportunity to observe a range of flying styles and talents.

At one time or another, most of us had occasion to take an F-4 up for a test flight. After repair service, an aircraft sometimes needed to be put through the motions, including supersonic flight. On a normal flight with either an external centerline fuel tank or bombs and rockets hanging under the wings, supersonic flight was not permitted, but test flights were usually flown "clean." On one test ride, my front-seater and I decided that after breaking the sound barrier (a requirement of that test flight), we'd see how fast we *could* go. A Machmeter indicates your speed in relation to the speed of sound. I was piloting. I climbed to about thirty thousand feet, lowered the nose, and moved the throttles into afterburner. We got our little bump as we went through Mach 1. We continued to accelerate until our speed was Mach 2.4, over sixteen hundred miles per hour.

"SITTING ALERT" IN KOREA was not practice. It was the real thing. I look back on that time—my four-day slots every few weeks in Korea—with a kind of amazement. No one expected that we would really drop a nuclear bomb on Russia. On the other hand we were prepared to do just that—or thought we were. At any time while we were sleeping in the alert shack, or playing Ping-Pong or cards there, or making audiotapes from the large selection of LPs, the Klaxon could go off.

When the Klaxon sound came blaring through the bullhorns, we scrambled and then ran for the crew trucks waiting outside with keys in the ignition. Four pilots to a truck. There would be two trucks, eight pilots for four airplanes. This was during the cold war. We assumed each time was practice, but we could never be absolutely sure until we were in our cranked aircraft listening to coded instructions on our radio. In our flight packets were maps with a Russian target clearly marked. Our helmets were fitted with gold-plated sun visors to protect our vision when our bomb detonated. I don't remember the particular targets near the city I was always slated to bomb, Vladivostok. But our four aircraft were possibly on the way to kill thousands of innocent people. People who'd never lifted a finger to harm me—and never would.

And if nuclear war came, hundreds of other aircraft were about to take off—from both sides.

My antimilitary inclinations in the late 1960s, and those of many of my buddies, took a gentle form. In Japan my refrigerator in the BOQ was decorated with a large peace symbol. On my wall was a poster of Snoopy, from *Peanuts,* who danced in hippie attire above the quotation "Groovy." Another poster had these words under a big flower: "War is not healthy for children and other living things." We were split in our thinking: While some of us would never have considered leaving the Air Force or not going to war when called, we felt a hazy empathy with the antiwar movement back in the States. But our Air Force culture allowed no discussion of the topic. Clearly, others of us would be adamantly opposed to the antiwar movement.

The nearest I came to nonmacho personal statements at Yokota were found on my refrigerator—about thirty quotations written in red Magic Marker: "People is people, but a frog is a friend forever." "Everything is mighty comfortable on a raft." "Jesus was a nonconformist."

As far as I know, I was the only English major in the group. In Korea I took an on-base English course on Jonathan Swift and Samuel Johnson. My dream, beyond my five years in the Air Force, was to return to North Carolina and teach high school English. None of my pilot buddies understood. And besides all that, I was a would-be poet. I was confident in my own abilities—and in those of a popular poet named Rod McKuen. To real poets, McKuen was the quintessential fake. But I didn't know that then. I had bought and read McKuen's book *Listen to the Warm.* It was a wildly popular best seller.

One night while on alert, several pilots sat quietly in the card room as I read a few of McKuen's poems aloud. The pilots had been chosen carefully: my front-seater, Sean Tuddle, twenty-seven and already married three times; Fireball Kelly, who'd once escaped from an F-4 that was burning on the ground; and Cam Knight, the "bubble check" front-seater. As they sometimes say in graduate English classes, we "explicated."

"I like that 'hidden country of your smile,'" said Cam.

"Why?" said Fireball.

"I don't know. I just do. Read that part again."

I read it again.

"What the hell does that mean?" asked Fireball.

"It's just a way of saying 'mysterious smile' without saying 'mysterious smile,'" I said.

"Why can't he say 'mysterious smile'?"

"Well, he can. It's just that he doesn't want to use a cliché. He wants to make it new and different."

"Cliché. Ha-ha."

"'Hidden country of your smile' is a hell of a lot better," said Sean. "Use your imagination, Fireball."

"I just don't know what's wrong with 'mysterious smile.' 'Hidden country' could be anything. Hell, it might even be 'hidden country.' Cliché, my ass."

And it went on like this for a while. But just that once. Explicating poetry didn't catch on.

I tried to learn poker, a popular pastime while we were sitting alert, but I was slow and untrained, and these guys played hardball. After saying "Clover leaves or shovels?" instead of "Clubs or spades?" I was escorted from the room by glares. But I did get a few of us noncardlayers onto the game Botticelli. You guess the identity of a famous person with the only initial clue being the last letter of his or her last name. We played for hours at a time while sitting alert, waiting to carry out our part of Armageddon.

In Korea we sometimes flew over the ocean just out from a popular beach and, fuel permitting, performed aerobatics at a safe distance from the beachgoers, hoping they were enjoying the show.

My favorite maneuver was a four-point aileron roll. Flying straight ahead, I pulled the nose up about ten degrees and slammed the stick to the right (or the left) and then quickly back to center so that the aircraft paused with the wings perpendicular to the ground; then another slam and pause, leaving me inverted, with wings parallel to the ground; then another slam and pause, with wings again perpendicular to the ground; and then another, bringing me back where I'd started, flying straight and level. If it came out about right, I'd do another roll, perhaps an eight-point roll, all the while imagining what it looked like from the ground, certain that the beachgoers appreciated the performance. It never occurred to me to think otherwise.

Other than participating in unauthorized dogfights, we normally stayed within all flying guidelines. Safety issues were hammered in through lectures and notices that followed all accidents and incidents (little accidents) Air Force–wide.

Occasionally one of our flying infractions occurred in front of the wrong person. My good friends Johnny Hobbs, a front-seater, and Bob Padget ("Poo"), his backseater, were preflighting their F-4 after refueling at Kunsan Air Base in Korea when an F-101 performed an afterburner climb-out on takeoff.

The ground crewman asked Johnny, "Will your airplane do that?"

Johnny, not knowing that an Air Force general was watching takeoffs, said something like, "Oh, I think it might."

On takeoff, Johnny and Poo not only did a burner climb (permissible), but at a few thousand feet up, still in afterburner, they performed a slow 360-degree roll (not permissible). The general saw this, went inside, and got on the phone, and when Johnny and Poo landed at Osan they were told to report to our commander, Colonel Bennington.

With a general looking over his shoulder, Colonel Bennington was in something of a tight spot. He took Johnny and Poo off flight status and sent them home to Japan to await a reprimand or a court-martial or something— something bad.

Grounded at Yokota, Johnny and Poo partied. And partied,

and partied. They'd been there for about a week when a North Korean aircraft shot down an American military aircraft (in April 1969) off the coast of South Korea, near the border with North Korea.

All of us flying F-4s at Osan were issued North Korean target maps. We held combat briefings. Armament would be conventional, not nuclear. I remember that my frontseater, Sean Tuddle, and I were scheduled to be number four in a flight of four in a large contingent of aircraft. This was not good. We would be the last of the four aircraft to drop bombs on the same target, and by the time number four came in, the guns below would be blazing and would likely be more accurate than when number one rolled in.

Besides being ready to fly combat missions from Osan, members of our squadron were now flying two aircraft in shifts in a large racetrack pattern off the northern coast of South Korea—twenty-four hours a day. These new missions were boring, though tense. Our radar was constantly scanning the coastline, ready and waiting for an attack from North Korean fighter aircraft. Sitting there, armed, we were in effect daring the North Koreans to attack us. Finally, after years of training, I was close to combat. We'd fly the racetrack for about two hours until we were low on fuel, and then we'd refuel from a C-135 tanker and fly another two hours before being relieved by two fresh aircraft. I remember looking down at the ocean far below, wondering what it would be like if we were attacked. And since they had just shot down one of our planes, why wouldn't they try it again?

Johnny and Poo were still in Japan, partying. But given the emergency, they were quietly placed back on flight status. We needed all the pilots we could muster. They caught a cargo hop to Osan. Luckily war did not come, and the tension gradually dissipated. In the hubbub, Johnny and Poo's transgression was somehow forgotten. They heard no more about their incident. We told them we had started a war to get them out of trouble.

"LET'S STEAL THE base commander's car," said Fireball. Several of us were sitting in the bar at Osan—not drinking, because we were on alert—listening to a radio broadcast that had just announced a fund-raising scheme for an off-base orphanage. Items could be confiscated, or a person could be voluntarily kidnapped and taken to the radio station. A ransom sum would be decided. If the owner of the item or a friend of the kidnappee called the station and pledged a ransom from a base organization, then the location of the confiscated item would be revealed or the kidnapped person would be released.

A new base commander, after a few weeks of command in mid-1969, was threatening to change the dress rules at the officer's club. His plan was to ban flight suits in the officer's club after 5:00 p.m. In both Japan and Korea—and on any other air base, as far as we knew—a pilot could go directly to the club in his flight suit and unwind after a flight. At any time of day.

In ten minutes we were driving in our alert truck by the base commander's residence, which was on top of a hill in the middle of the base. Big house. And sitting placidly in his driveway, just outside of his garage, was his car—a big black sedan. We'd had to drive through a guarded gate to get to his residence, and we would have to drive back out the same way. But because we were in a U.S. Air Force alert truck and an officer was driving (the other two of us were hidden down on the back floorboard), our truck had been saluted and waved on in. We didn't know if driving the general's car *out* would be so easy.

I was selected to see if keys were in the ignition. I walked casually to the car and looked in the window. Yes—and the door was unlocked. I returned to our truck and told the boys. Piece of cake. Fireball and I approached the car, I got in and put the car in neutral, and then we pushed it out the driveway and into the street. I jumped in and cranked it as Fireball got on the floor in the backseat. Of course the guard at the gate knew this car. We hoped that he wouldn't stop us.

He didn't.

So where do you hide a general's car? It was a nice automobile. We drove around on base for a while. It was about 10:30 p.m. We found ourselves on a dead-end road that ended in a small field with trees. We drove out onto the field. The field was wet, and toward the trees it became very muddy. We drove the car into the mud. The alert truck stood by in case the Klaxon sounded and we were called to nuclear war. The car was good and stuck.

"We shouldn't have two sets of footprints leaving the car," said Fireball from the backseat.

"Why?"

"Conspiracy. They'll figure it out. It needs to seem like a one-man job."

"How are we going to leave one set of footprints?"

"You get out. I climb on your back."

"You just don't want to get your damn boots muddy. I think we ought to—"

By this time I was out of the car with my back to the front door. Fireball was climbing on.

When we got back to the club, I called the radio station to let them know what was up. I told the announcer that the base commander's car had been stolen and it seemed to me that the ransom should be very high. He agreed and then asked me what unit I was with.

"What unit?" I answered.

"Yes. What unit?"

"Why do you need to know that?"

"We're keeping records. We just need to know."

"Do I have to tell you?"

"Well, sure."

"What if I don't?"

"Then I guess you'll have to work all this out on your own. In order to make the announcement on the air, we have to have all the information."

"Okay. The Thirty-fifth Tac Fighter Squadron."

"What's the ransom amount?"

"A hundred bucks."

I went back into the bar and sat down with my buddies. In about five minutes we heard this announcement: "And we've just got this one in. The base commander's car has been stolen by members of the Thirty-fifth Tactical Fighter Squadron . . ."

Everybody looked at me. "Why the hell did you say who we were?!" somebody said.

". . . and the sum of the ransom we're placing on the car can be decided by our generous commander, but our suggested amount is one hundred dollars. Hats off to members of the Thirty-fifth Tac Fighter Squadron."

We waited for the hammer to fall, but it never did. And the new flight suit rule never went through, though our effort probably wasn't the reason.

We did hear words from the base commander on another occasion, a month or so later.

Near a side door to the officer's club at Osan were two parking spaces marked ALERT VEHICLE. I'd never seen any vehicle except ours parked in these spaces. One night, as we approached the officer's club, I noticed a car in one of the reserved spaces. An alert truck would have to park elsewhere. I was thinking, Who the hell is that? A closer inspection told me: it was the same car we'd kidnapped. Rather than do the brave thing—find the general and ask him to move his car—I phoned the air police and told them about the unauthorized car in an alert-vehicle parking place at the officer's club. They asked for my name. I thought, I don't have a damn thing to hide; I am so *right* on this and he is so blatantly wrong.

Next day, a meeting was called. I remember that Major Newsome, one of our senior officers, was in charge of the meeting. He said word had come down that a lieutenant in our squadron had reported the base commander for illegal parking and that the base commander had met with our squadron commander and operations officers and, by golly, so-and-so and so-and-so. I remember only one phrase from the speech: the base commander had said that he had "slept under enough wings" in his time not to be called to task about where he parked his car. After that meeting, my front-seater, Sean, was called in and told to have a meeting with me, the culprit, and lay down the law. Sean told me about all this with a smile—at the bar—and said, "We've had our meeting. And next time don't say who you are, dummy."

MAJOR DODGE, THE COMMANDER of the air police squadron on base at Osan, was coming to know several of us by name. Incidents of loud noise and rowdiness had brought us together.

I was rooming with Johnny Hobbs in the Osan Air Base BOQ, and on the night in question I had decided to stay in our room, alone, because I was on crutches from a motorcycle accident. (Two of us owned dirt bikes and I'd flipped mine.) I was talking into my portable tape recorder at about eleven o'clock when a group of nine tipsy pilots, including Johnny, Jake Brooks (with a guitar), Ted Graham, and Fireball Kelly walked into the room. They had just placed an Army officer's motorcycle in the third-floor hallway. (In Korea we shared a three-story barracks with Army officers.)

The boys made themselves comfortable and we started singing "Long, Tall Texan," a popular song of the time. I pressed the record button on my handheld tape recorder. A box of brownies that had come by mail that day was passed around. Someone threw one. Another. Several more. More singing. Giggling. Peanut shells littered the floor. Someone stood, stepped on a brownie, then another. Fireball *stomped* a brownie. Funniest thing.

A knock on the door.

On the tape you hear the door creak open and then, "Staff Sergeant Cheek, sir. Air police. Major Dodge has authorized me to place you under house arrest until further notice."

Whoops.

I stayed on my bed, and the tape recorder picked up pieces of the conversation. Members of our group argued with Sergeant Cheek, laughing the whole time.

"We can't *leave* the *room?* We can't go to our *own rooms?*"

"No, sir. Those are my orders."

Jake Brooks had a piece of paper and a pencil. "What's your name, sergeant?"

"Cheek, sir."

"How do you spell that? Is it C-h-e-e-k or C-h-e-a-k?"

Sergeant Cheek didn't see the humor.

"Two *e*'s, sir."

"Can I make a phone call?" asked Johnny. (There was a pay phone in the hall.)

"No, sir."

"Wait a minute! We're allowed one phone call."

"You have to stay in the room, sir."

"Oh, my God, we're under house arrest."

We settled back into the room and started singing again: "Well, I'm a long, tall Texan. I ride a big white horse."

On the recorder you hear talking, laughing, more singing, then another knock on the door. The singing continues. The door creaks open.

It was Major Dodge. He stepped in. An unlit cigarette hung from his lips, and a pair of pants that Johnny had thrown on a whim at someone else clipped the unlit cigarette in his mouth, so that the broken half dangled from the half still in his lips. We kept singing as if Major Dodge didn't exist. "Yes, I'm a long, tall Texan . . ." I think I was the only one looking at him. He seemed startled, as if he had forgotten what he was going to say. He glanced around the room at nine singing pilots, then stepped back outside and closed the door. It was a scene for the movies—and I had only a tape recorder.

When the singing finally stopped, someone in the room shouted, "Sergeant Cheek!"

"Yes, sir" (from the hall).

"Can we come out now?"

"No, sir, you're still under house arrest."

Ted Graham stood, walked over to the window by my bed, where I was propped up on pillows, and opened it, and when he climbed through, stepping out onto the ground, I started a running commentary into the tape recorder: "There are now only eight of us in the room. Graham just left through the—whoops, now there are seven of us . . . six."

In the background you hear singing, talking, and laughing, though it's losing force.

Jake was sitting in a chair, playing guitar and singing, Johnny was on his bed, singing, and I was sitting on my bed, counting into the recorder mic. "Four . . . three. There are only three of us left in the room."

If I hadn't played the tape several times after the event, I'm sure I wouldn't remember what happened next; nor would I remember the details of the foregoing. (Sadly, the tape is now long lost.)

Johnny went to sleep, or passed out, and in the quiet you hear Jake say faintly, "Well, I guess we'd better clean up."

He and I got down on the floor and began cleaning up peanut hulls and brownies, putting them in a trash can between us. The recorder was on the floor near him. He started a commentary, pretending he was our spokesperson, testifying before a military judge. His speech was slightly slurred, but spirited. "These men are here today, Your Honor, not proud, but contrite." (Long pause.) "They were unaware that their somewhat raucous—though innocent—social behavior would have any, even one single solitary, unsavory consequence. These are *good* men, Your Honor, and I can only hope that you will recognize that they are the backbone of our American armed forces and that you will—"

The door creaks open: our commander, Colonel Bennington. He walks over.

I remember looking up at him standing there. From my perspective down on the floor, he looked tall, even though he was a short man. He asks a question, but his voice is so quiet you can't make it out on the tape.

Jake responds: "Brownies, sir."

Last Flights

OUR LITTLE BLUES BAND's main audience for the afternoon and night music sessions was two bachelors who lived with us in BOQ 16: Johnny Hobbs and Rob Stedman. Johnny liked the music of Mose Allison (especially his rendition of "One Room Country Shack") and any number of tunes from Sonny Terry and Brownie McGhee.

Rob, a shy midwesterner with a crew cut, the only jazz aficionado among us, enjoyed talking about any kind of music and owned a more extensive collection of tapes and records than any of us. He had a kind of swaying, bow-legged walk and was slightly pigeon toed, and when he handled things, his elbows stuck out and his index fingers always seemed to be held up and curved somehow—the mannerisms of a left-handed baseball pitcher. You would not have been surprised to see him go into a stretch at any moment, check first base, and then try the pickoff. His demeanor and spirit were those of a gentle uncle.

Rob lived on the first floor of BOQ 16 in the middle of

the party zone. But he didn't party much because of his devotion to Linda, who was waiting for him at home in Florida.

We bought Rob a bottle of champagne to help us all celebrate as soon as he landed from his last F-4 flight. We planned to meet him at the airplane. We didn't always go to this much trouble, but this was not only Rob's last flight in the F-4, but his last flight in the Air Force. He wasn't just going home; he was going home to marry Linda. She'd visited Rob in Yokota and we all liked her a lot.

That last mission was to be a simulated bombing mission, involving a pop-up bombing maneuver. Four aircraft, in single file, would fly at low level toward a mountain and then at the last minute pop up to bomb a target on the other side of the mountain. The target, I assume, was straight ahead, unlike most targets, which were usually approached from a ninety-degree angle high above the target. The problem was to make the transition from a climbing attitude straight at the target (over the mountain) to a dive. The flight leader briefed a kind of barrel-roll roll-in on the target. Had I been in the flight, I would have been surprised because I'd never heard of such a thing, much less practiced it.

Rob and Davie Long, Rob's front-seater, were number two. Apparently the lead's aircraft got very slow on the maneuver, and before Davie initiated the same maneuver, he had to reduce speed to keep adequate distance behind the lead aircraft. Apparently the combination of a strange maneuver and being too slow caused Rob's F-4 to stall at low altitude, perhaps while inverted, and then to crash, killing both pilots.

A pilot in an aircraft behind Rob's reported that only Rob ejected, and his parachute opened, but he drifted into the fireball made by the crash of his aircraft.

An investigation found that fire had burned Rob's para-chute shroud cords, releasing him from his parachute—too high in the air for him to survive the impact.

I was asked to be Rob's summary courts officer, mean-ing it would be my job to inform Rob's family of his death, to gather his belongings together—in short, to take care of things for him.

I sent a telegram to Linda and then wrote her a letter.

The officer at the morgue gave me Rob's belongings, including his boots, which were torn at the seams from impact, and his watch, which was stopped at 4:17. The morgue officer asked me if I wanted to see Rob.

I said no.

Linda wrote me back. I remember these words from her letter: "I never before knew the meaning of despair."

SIX OTHER PILOTS died in aircraft accidents at Yokota during my eighteen-month assignment, but none were friends. At least two more who were friends died in noncombat crashes within a few years. Another pilot from Yokota, Dave Grant, upgraded to the front seat, went to Vietnam, became a POW, and was released in 1973.

After Rob died, Jake Brooks said to me, "I get his radio."

I looked at him funny.

"Oh," he said, "you haven't been to Vietnam, have you? I was kidding. That's how we handled it."

It made sense. I realized that any reaction—from me—

to Mike Tressler's death, early on in my Japan tour, had been muted. And now with Rob's death, a much closer friend, I'd somehow been unable, perhaps unwilling, to do anything that resembled mourning.

As we finished our F-4 days in Japan, I awaited word about my new assignment. I'd be going to Southeast Asia for sure, but in what airplane?

Staying in the F-4 meant upgrading to the front seat and remaining in the Air Force two years beyond my five-year commitment, so I applied for an OV-10, mainly because of the buzz about this new little twin-engine turboprop aircraft. It looked odd but was very fast and fully aerobatic (meaning you could fly it upside down). The T-37, T-38, and F-4 had been aerobatic, and I didn't want a step-down.

The OV-10, a tandem two-seater, a reconnaissance and "strike control" aircraft, would get me into the front seat, alone. The OV-10 backseat was used for instruction only. The mythology of the World War I and II aces, who flew alone, was still strong.

Before my last flight in the F-4, news came: OV-10 to SEA.

PART 4

(1970)

Preparing for Combat

War Fever or Flying Fever?

I CAME HOME FROM Japan in the early spring of 1970. My schedule for the remainder of the year would be as follows: I'd spend three months, from March to May, in air-gunnery training in the T-33, an old jet trainer, at Cannon Air Force Base in Clovis, New Mexico, in preparation for three months, from June to August, checking out the OV-10 at Hurlburt Field, Fort Walton Beach, Florida. In September I'd go to the Philippines for five days of jungle-survival training, and in October I'd be assigned to Southeast Asia for a year, as a "FAC."

FAC meant forward air controller. A FAC directed fighter-bombers against enemy ground targets. My main combat job would be to shoot a white phosphorus smoke rocket at a target and then radio information to fighter-bomber aircraft. When the rocket hit the ground, smoke billowed up from the impact, and once the smoke was sighted by fighter-bombers high overhead, my job would be to say exactly where the target was in relation to the smoke, and then clear the bombers (give them permission) to drop bombs on the target, which might or might not be clearly visible. After the fighter-bombers left, I would visually assess the damage and report that to headquarters.

The OV-10 could also shoot high-explosive rockets and strafe with four internally mounted machine guns if necessary during a battle or rescue attempt.

In Southeast Asia we'd be stationed in South Vietnam, where the mission would be to direct bombing during ground battles between troops, *or* in Thailand, where our mission would be to direct bombing of the Ho Chi Minh Trail in Laos. No U.S. or South Vietnamese troops were allowed in Laos (or so I then believed), thus there would be no close air support of troops there.

As to my thoughts about the war, they were about the same as they'd been several years earlier. I realized this when I was home in 1970 and read the words of a letter I'd written from Laredo in the summer of 1967. My father had advised me *not* to go into the military. He had never been with me to an airport. He was not a pacifist, but he had little room in his life for risk. From early on he didn't want me to play football, wanted me to stay out of deep water. He himself would not board an aircraft or a boat, nor would he drive a car in the mountains.

My mother and aunt, who wrote to me often, underlined words for humorous effect—old sayings, malapropisms, and so forth—and I'd picked up the habit.

Here's the letter from flight training in 1967:

Well Hello,

Hope all is going well at home. I'm doing just fine.

The trip this weekend [a solo cross-country flight] was really nice. California and the Sierra Mountains, etc., were all beautiful from the air. I took a bunch of pictures and will be sending home a bunch when I get them back.

The yearbook is coming along pretty slowly right now. We've really got a lot of work to do before Sept. 15th. That's when we should complete our layout to send in to the publisher. I've got 3 or 4 guys helping me with it.

All that food from the garden is really something—it sure sounds good.

<u>Daddy,</u> it would be better to talk to you about this and maybe we can talk it over in Oct. but all I can do now is write:

I have no idea now about what my assignment will be when I get out of here in about 6 or 8 weeks. I will write down the list of airplanes I want to fly in order of preference, for example: (1) F-100, (2) F-102, (3) F-101, (4) F-4C, (5) C-130, (6) C-141. Then those in charge of assignments will give me the highest on my list that they can—<u>depending on openings.</u> Now of all the planes I can put down, some of each kind are being used in Viet Nam. That's not my choice, that's just the way it is: The Air Force is using some of just about every type of plane they have in Viet Nam. So I very well might get an airplane of a type that's being used in Viet Nam; however, I could very easily be assigned to Germany or England or Florida or even Virginia instead of Viet Nam. (Because not <u>all</u> of every type is being used in Viet Nam.)

On the phone you didn't ask me how I felt about going to Viet Nam. I think it's very important how I feel about it (<u>and I know you do</u>) and I've given it very much serious thought and heard and read about many different viewpoints. Captain Dunning spent a tour (1 year) in Viet Nam. Also there are about 5 instructors in our flight who have been and there are many other instructors on base who have been. Some missions in Viet Nam consist of carrying supplies to Army camps. Some missions consist of carrying medical supplies. Major Stricker, who is a member at Capt. Dunning's church, flew medical supplies, food, etc., around to different villages. There are also reconnaissance missions (picture taking). Then of course there are the combat missions. Some Viet Nam tours last 1 yr. and some last 6 months and some last for 100 missions. At present, no pilot has to serve more than one tour except on rare occasions or when he volunteers.

I do not agree with everything the United States is doing in V.N. At least I don't agree with the <u>way</u> some things are being done, but I <u>do</u> believe we should be there because I have <u>studied</u> the reasons we are there and I know the basic cause of the trouble and <u>very simply</u> stated it's this: Those leaders who are behind the communists are determined to do everything possible to take over Viet Nam, then Thailand, then other countries in Asia, Africa, South America, Latin America, and the final goal is the U.S. That's <u>exactly</u> what they want (can and might do it) and what they are

fighting for. And thanks to UNC and what I've read I
know enough about communism to understand that
it's <u>bad.</u>

If I thought that this has nothing to do with me and
that I should stay away from it I would stop flying tomorrow and say, "Give me another job. I don't want to
take a chance on going to Viet Nam." And that's exactly
what they would do. They would relieve me of my
flying duties, and I <u>would not</u> have to worry about
<u>going</u> to Viet Nam. It's called SIE: self-initiated elimi-
nation, and I have that right to quit.

I cannot do that tho, because I would be going
against what I <u>believe</u> and what I <u>feel.</u> I'm <u>not</u> <u>afraid</u> of
going to Viet Nam if it comes to that, and if I <u>said</u> I was
afraid of going and if I tried to get out of going, then I'd
be living a <u>lie</u> and I can't do that.

I hope you sorta see how I feel. I respect your ideas
very much and am very much interested in what you
think about what I do. Likewise I want you to see and
understand the way I feel. I'm not going to <u>try</u> to get a
Viet Nam assignment, but if I'm given a Viet Nam assignment I'm not going to say, "Oh, no, I don't want to
go." I'll simply say, "I'm ready." And the reason I'll say
that is because it's the <u>truth</u>. I <u>am</u> ready if it's necessary
for me to go. I'm not afraid.

XXXXXXXXXXXXXXXXX [something crossed out].
Oh, well, enough about all that. I might just end up
back here in Laredo as an instructor. Frankly, I think 3
more years (instructor assignments are 3 yrs.) here
would drive me out of my head. It has advantages tho.

Listen, Daddy, be sure to vote <u>Republican</u> in '68

and maybe this country will get straightened out and finish up in Viet Nam for good. I've been telling you all along that Republican is the only way to go. Ha.

We'll talk it all over in October.

Your son,
Clyde

P.S. I sure feel better after writing this!

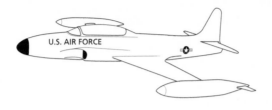

T-33 Air-to-Ground Gunnery

PRELIMINARY GUNNERY TRAINING in the T-33 would teach us how to shoot rockets and drop practice bombs from a front seat. We'd also learn about problems that fighter-bomber pilots might encounter on bombing runs in Southeast Asia while we, as FACs, directed them from the OV-10. Those of us who had already flown fighters were not exempt from this training.

Among the T-33 trainees were older pilots who'd flown all kinds of airplanes, including single-seat fighters. There were also youngsters straight out of pilot training, and a few of us who'd flown backseat in the F-4. The T-33 was the trainer version of the then-ancient P-80, the first operational jet fighter (1945) in U.S. history.

My having to do this T-33 gunnery training was like Brer Rabbit's being thrown into the briar patch. I knew I was going to love it because it meant flying alone, flying formation, and flying bombing-range patterns.

A range pattern works like a traffic pattern: the aircraft

flies in a big rectangle and drops bombs or shoots rockets or strafes with machine guns during one of the legs of the rectangle.

The rocket and bomb patterns are from higher altitudes than traffic patterns for landing, and the strafing pattern takes the aircraft closer to the ground than either bomb or rocket patterns. After bombs are released or rockets or bullets are shot at a make-believe target, the aircraft comes out of its dive and climbs to pattern altitude to fly around for the next ordnance (jargon for bombs, rockets, or bullets) delivery. The target for bombs and rockets is a large bull's-eye on the ground. Observers in a tower nearby (but not too near) measure the accuracy of each bomb or rocket and call out, "Fifteen at six" (meaning the bomb or rocket hit fifteen meters to the six o'clock position of the bull's-eye), "Thirty at nine," and so forth. And if a bomb or rocket hits the bull's-eye, the pilot hears, "Shack."

The target for bullets from machine guns was a soccer-goal-like device that automatically counted the number of bullets entering the goal.

Groups of us in our class were assigned to instructors. Mine was a Dustin Hoffman look-alike named Riley Porter, a captain, and an instructor who loved to laugh and call his students "plumbers." "You're a plumber, Edgerton," he might say after a flight in which I'd made a mistake. "Is he a plumber or what?" he'd say to other student pilots. But Porter was not a screamer. He was the only humorist I ever had as an instructor. It was all fun and games. But intense. We had to learn to fly this old bird in a week or so and then within the remainder of our three months become proficient at air-to-ground gunnery.

The T-33 was a clunker, slow on the uptake. It would finally get to moving along on takeoff roll, with its single jet engine wide open (no afterburner), and then lift into the air only after a long roll. It handled well in the air, but its technology was archaic. For example, fuel fed into a central fuel tank from three separate feeder tanks—one at a time—and when fuel was about to run out of one, a red light came on and a manually operated switch turned a valve so that another tank could feed. A buddy forgot to make a switch one day, and the engine flamed out; he couldn't get the engine restarted, and ejected safely.

After we were each checked out in the T-33, we flew to the gunnery range in four-ship formation unless mechanical problems (common in the old T-33) forced one of us to abort the flight.

Captain Porter had four air-to-ground gunnery students, old and young. When a four-ship went to the range, we each flew alone in our airplane except for the lead aircraft. Captain Porter would ride in the backseat of that aircraft, where there was a second set of flight controls.

The pilots and instructor always met for a flight briefing about ninety minutes before takeoff, talked over every detail of the upcoming flight, and then caught a van to the flight line. The routine was the same as ever. After preflighting our aircraft (we were assigned aircraft by the numbers printed on the tail), we each strapped in with the help of an enlisted man whose job was to be with us until we taxied away.

At this point in my flying career—I'd been flying for about three years—I was confident, and stepping out of the van and facing a jet aircraft, even a clunky old T-33, that was about to be mine for more than an hour, made my blood rise. I'd say hello to the airman assigned to the aircraft; look over the aircraft logbook, which recorded recent maintenance; ask the airman any pertinent questions; and check the general condition of the aircraft, including landing gear, landing gear struts, wheels, guns, bomb canisters, and my ejection seat. This walk-around was not unlike that walk-around in the Cherokee 140, back when I first started flying with Mr. Vaughn. He would have said, "Well, yeah"—sniff—"pretty much the same thing except for the guns and ammo. But you've got to use that checklist."

The general procedure on the bombing range was exactly as it had been in the F-4 except that I was now up front. Solo.

An adjustable bomb sight, or "pipper," was mounted against the windshield in front of the pilot. It was set according to the proposed speed, angle of dive, and altitude at release of ordnance. In theory the bomb, rocket, or bullets would be released or shot when the aircraft was at an exact spot in the air, at an exact speed and angle, and would thus hit the target in the crosshairs. In practice we often released high, low, fast, slow, or at too shallow or steep an angle. Back then, no instrument indicated angle of dive, and no laser beam directed the bomb. Additionally the wind might be blowing more forcefully than forecast by the tower. So after release, upon hearing a bad score, I'd have to figure out the problem. For example, if the angle, speed, and altitude of release were accurate, and the pipper was on the bull's-eye at release, but my bomb was off to the right, then I'd likely decide that the wind was stronger from the left than had been forecast; and so on the next drop I'd aim at a spot on the ground to offset the direction and velocity of the wind. Wind had more effect on bombs than on rockets and more effect on rockets than on bullets.

We soon discovered that simultaneously doing all of the following on the gunnery range in the T-33 was not simple: staying in the pattern, not lagging behind or crowding the previous aircraft, resetting the bomb sight as necessary, monitoring the fuel so that when fuel was low in one feeder tank, the next tank was selected, adjusting dive angles, adjusting airspeed, making the correct radio calls at the correct time—all while watching out for other aircraft.

The need for a forward air controller in combat became clear. He'd verbally clear a fighter-bomber to drop bombs on each pass, one after the other, and serve as the fighter-bomber pilot's eyes and ears.

One day I completed my T-33 preflight, cranked up, closed my canopy, switched on my radio, and waited for the lead aircraft to initiate a radio check-in.

"Silver Flight, radio check," called lead.

"Silver Two."

"Silver Three."

"Silver Four," I called.

I was about to experience the pure aloneness and exhilarating tension that was possible in a four-ship-formation flight. I knew the airplane well by then, and I was able to fly nearly flawless formation. After we were cleared onto the range, I'd fly the range patterns, getting my aircraft situated above the target, which would be at nine o'clock low—it's like looking from a very high building down at something on the ground (not straight down but at a thirty- to forty-five-degree angle). Then I'd pull the throttle to idle, roll into a ninety-degree-plus banked left turn, pull the nose around as it fell below the horizon line until I felt almost aligned with a straight path across the ground up to the target, and then abruptly roll out of my turn. I'd be in a wings-level dive toward the target. From the cockpit I'd see the target out in front of me, and the nose of the aircraft would be tracking across the ground straight toward it. At this point in the process I might see that the target was a few degrees left or right of a straight line from my aircraft nose to the target, and I'd make a quick correction while checking my altimeter.

Pipper tracking toward target.

Altitude, three hundred feet from drop.

Just right.

Pickle (meaning "press the bomb button on the stick grip").

I'd then pull about four g's out of the bottom of my dive to a nose-high climb attitude, push the throttles to 100 percent, dip a wing, and look back over my shoulder at the target below. Was it a shack? Yes! The tower operator announced, "Silver Four, shack." I'd write down my score on a card that was clamped onto a stiff board attached to my right knee with Velcro.

After we'd expended bombs, rockets, and bullets, we'd all come home and I'd fly the traffic pattern and land. We'd meet in the van, talk about it all, laugh, go to the officer's club, and talk some more.

But just after engine start, on this particular day, my engine temperature was out of bounds. I quickly shut down the engine and, before turning off the battery, called lead: "Silver Lead, Silver Four."

"Go ahead, Silver Four."

"Engine problems. Aborting."

"Roger, Four. If you can get a spare, we'll see you at the range."

I had to move fast. I wanted to catch them *on the way* to the range.

A spare was available. I found the aircraft, did a quick but thorough preflight check, started the engine, checked instruments, lowered the canopy, and taxied out. I pictured the others at least a third of the way to the range, flying in a three-ship formation. I *hated* to miss a minute of formation flying.

After being cleared onto the runway for takeoff, I took off and turned to the heading that would take me to the range. I opened the throttle—pushed it to the wall. If I caught them before they got to the range, Captain Porter would be impressed, as would the others.

The F-4 that I'd been flying for two years had two powerful jet engines, and the throttles were side by side. The throttle handles came up out of the left console and moved forward or backward together, fitting into my gloved left hand as would two short, stubby gearshifts. In the F-4 (as well as in the T-37 and T-38) there was always that feel of *two* throttles, the knowledge that if an engine failed, you'd simply pull that throttle all the way back, click it over a little hump, thus shutting down the fuel and ignition supply, and then continue flying with the other engine. You wouldn't get the normal power response, but you'd have enough power to fly home and land safely.

But in the T-33, just that *one* throttle rested under my left hand, and that felt odd. Additionally the T-33 had only a fraction of the power of the F-4, and on that day she seemed unusually slow on takeoff and I was in a hurry. I kept the aircraft at a low altitude, flying over New Mexico flatlands. Flying low, I could enjoy the speed. In spite of the relative lack of power, the old T-33 scooted right along once she got moving.

I caught up as the three-ship formation lazily entered a racetrack pattern to wait for entry onto the range.

Once on the range, we all flew our patterns, made our calls, dropped our practice bombs, shot our rockets and guns. During join-up, after the last pass, Captain Porter called over the radio, "Silver Flight. Fuel check."

This meant each pilot had to call on the radio the amount of fuel left in his tank. Why, hell, I hadn't even thought about fuel. I'd switched my tanks at appropriate times. But we always had enough, didn't we? We'd usually try to land with over two hundred pounds of fuel, enough to easily get us to any of the nearest civilian fields in case the runway at Cannon was closed because of an emergency, and it took about two hundred pounds to fly back to the base from the bomb range. Therefore, after the range flying, we each needed in the vicinity of five hundred pounds for a comfortable flight home—four hundred minimum.

I looked at my fuel gauge. Silver 2 and 3 called in comfortable numbers. I was embarrassed, startled, and suddenly uneasy. "Silver Four. One niner zero pounds." I could feel my neck and ears getting red.

Captain Porter radioed, "Say again, number four."

"One niner zero pounds."

Captain Porter immediately gave me a heading to fly and told me an altitude and power setting, a power setting that he knew would be the most fuel efficient. He called ahead to the airfield and declared an emergency. Fire trucks would be waiting, just in case. But if I crashed, I probably wouldn't burn—from loose fuel, anyway.

Porter asked me again for a fuel reading, as he would several more times. He had decided I would land before the others, and not from a conventional overhead pattern. I'd fly straight in, and to assure that I was at proper altitudes and airspeeds all the way in, until just before touchdown I'd fly on Captain Porter's wing. He'd make all the radio calls while flying the appropriate throttle setting and route.

At about a half mile from the runway, he told me to extend my gear and land straight ahead. He and I both knew I had to make the landing good. I couldn't afford a go-around. He broke away and would come around to land after the other two aircraft had safely landed behind me. It all went smoothly, and I touched down with enough fuel to taxi in and close my throttle. I completed my after-flight checklist, got out of the airplane, and waited for the van. I was the first pickup. I climbed in, and the van drove toward the other pilots, standing in a group. I was sitting inside the van on the bench that ran around its interior, my helmet in my lap, when Captain Porter stuck his head in the door.

"Edgerton. You plumber. You dumb-ass plumber. Take him on in," he said to the van driver. "We'll wait for the next van."

I rode in alone.

Captain Porter was unforgiving in the debriefing. How could a good pilot not check his fuel every thirty minutes? It was another of those cheap lessons. Seat belt, mile and minute ticks, takeoff trim, and now fuel check—lessons I'd now take on to Hurlburt Field, in Fort Walton Beach, Florida.

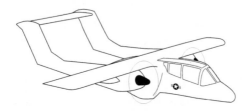

The OV-10

THE OV-10 WAS AN odd-looking bird. It sat nose low, tail high. Twin booms ran from the twin turboprop engines to the tail, where a high horizontal stabilizer (or tail wing) rested between two vertical stabilizers. This meant that it looked a bit like the old P-38, a famous World War II fighter. In fact the OV-10 was almost exactly half the weight (ten thousand pounds compared to about twenty thousand pounds), with half the horsepower of the P-38 (about fifteen hundred versus about three thousand). Because it was relatively fresh off the assembly line (1967), both the inside and the outside of the OV-10 looked and smelled new—not at all like the old, worn T-33s. The instrument panel was relatively simple. It was a two-seater, with tandem seats like a fighter, and had fighterlike flight controls—stick in the middle, throttles on the left.

In the F-4 and other jets I'd flown, the clear Plexiglas canopy over my head stopped at about my shoulders, so I could see above me, left and right, but not below me unless I banked my aircraft. With the OV-10, the Plexiglas canopy was like a jet canopy, clear overhead, but the base of it came around and down nearly to my butt on each side. Flying along, I could lean to the left or right and look almost straight down. It was designed for, among other tasks, reconnaissance.

Our job at Hurlburt Field was to get used to flying the OV-10 and to learn how to be a forward air controller.

SOMEHOW PROPELLER ENGINES seem friendlier than jet engines. They sound friendlier. And you *see* how the engine is working—you see the propeller, whereas with a jet engine you can only hear the noise.

The OV-10 was fully aerobatic, and flying aerobatics was part of our familiarization week. In the classroom we learned the aircraft's performance limits. In the air we learned the feel of those limits.

A main surprise was the OV-10's rapid acceleration. Its top speed was around three hundred miles an hour, and it could land quite slowly and stop very quickly. It was designed for short, rapidly built dirt landing strips.

The props on the OV-10 were reversible. When the throttles (called power levers in the OV-10) were pulled all the way back to idle, lifted, and pulled back even farther, over a little bump, the propellers would turn in their sockets so that they provided reverse thrust. This force, along with the brakes, brought the airplane to a quick stop after landing, and it was always fun to see just how quick. We'd have contests for the shortest landing distance.

After checking out in the OV-10, two of us, in different aircraft, with an instructor in one backseat, flew to a practice area and directed each other in simulated air strikes. We each carried practice bombs to drop when we were the pretend fighter-bomber.

If I was the FAC and the other guy was simulating being the fighter-bomber, I'd make sure I saw him and he saw me, and then I'd let him know that I was going to "mark the target." Say the other aircraft was Falcon 4 and I was Trapper 66.

"Falcon Four, this is Trapper Six Six. I have a tallyho [I see you]. I'm at your three o'clock position low. I'm above the big S in the road and I'm rocking my wings."

"Roger, Trapper Six Six, I have a tally. Falcon Four." (On an initial radio call it's customary for the calling party to end with his call sign—in this case, Falcon 4.)

"Roger, Falcon." (The number is often dropped after contact is established.) "Do you see the S in the road beneath me?"

"Roger that."

"Your target is that road. I'm in for a smoke." That meant I would shoot a smoke rocket to mark the target.

Generally, before shooting the rocket, the FAC set up his flight path so that the target was positioned off the left or right wing. Next came a ninety-degree turn and a dive toward the target from a predetermined altitude at a predetermined angle and airspeed. Controlling these variables increased the chances of an accurate smoke. But such planning was not always possible. I'd have a pipper setting (gun-sight setting), which would allow me to shoot an accurate rocket from a certain altitude and speed. I would roll in for the dive toward the road segment to be cut, my throttles in idle, and at the right instant I'd press a rocket-firing button on the hand grip of my flight stick. Then I'd pull up as quickly as possible because I would want to avoid ground fire. I'd move the throttles forward to 100 percent power, and as I climbed I would turn the aircraft one way and then the other, unpredictably (jinking, it was called) to prevent easy enemy gunnery tracking.

I would look back down over my shoulder (my nose would be pointed skyward) and see the smoke rising up from the ground near the area of the road that was supposed to be cut, and I'd make my next radio call: "Falcon. Do you have my smoke?"

"Affirmative."

"The target is the road, thirty meters north of my smoke." I would have missed the exact spot, which I knew from the coordinates I was assigned and from the description of the target, by thirty meters to the south. The procedure was complicated by the fact that I'd have to ensure that the fighter-bombers were flying over a safe area, and if I was directing them onto enemy troops, I'd have to be able to ensure that they did not attack friendly troops. "Falcon Four is cleared in." I'd clear each fighter-bomber for each pass if there were more than one. No bombs were to be dropped without the FAC's clearance. While the bomber dropped bombs, I'd have to remain clear of the bomber. I'd set up a figure-eight pattern near the target, sometimes directly over it, so that I could almost constantly monitor what was going on.

OUR TRAINING WOULD prepare us for air war over either Laos or Vietnam. To fly over Laos, we'd be stationed in Thailand. In Laos, large anti-aircraft guns were stationed along the Ho Chi Minh Trail to protect supplies being shipped (by truck, bicycle, and foot) from North Vietnam along the trail into South Vietnam. While we directed air strikes there, we would be required to stay at least forty-five hundred feet—almost a mile—above the ground to reduce the chances of being hit by fire from those guns.

In Vietnam, on the other hand, there were few large antiaircraft guns, but there was plenty of small-arms fire and plenty of north Vietnamese and Vietcong troops engaging Americans and South Vietnamese. FACs there often flew at treetop level, directing fighter-bomber fire onto enemy troops.

We were learning all of this in classes and by word of mouth at Hurlburt Field in Florida while we decided whether to request Vietnam or Thailand. In Vietnam we might be living in tents some of the time. From over Laos we'd be able to return to our Thailand base and our BOQ after each flight, and visit the officer's club for food and drink, but the mission there, because of the big guns along the trail, was considered more dangerous.

I was undecided and saw no need to hurry my decision.

BECAUSE JET FIGHTERS were stationed at nearby Eglin Air Force Base, we had to be on the lookout for them when we were flying to and from our practice missions. They almost always flew in pairs, a lead and a wingman, and the wingman often flew about thirty yards behind and perhaps fifty yards out from the side of the lead. We never worked with these fighters in simulated air strikes—we always worked with each other—but because they were around much of the time, we had to be careful to avoid collisions.

One day I was heading out from base alone at about forty-five hundred feet when all of a sudden, at exactly my altitude, from left to right, came a fighter, about fifty yards in front of me. As it zipped across, I thought, Where's the *other* one? With that, my whole windshield was filled with the other fighter, and my airplane jerked violently up and back down from the jet wash (the turbulent air following a jet). He barely—*just* barely—missed me. On landing, he reported that he thought he'd struck another aircraft that he hadn't seen until the last second.

Shaken, I flew the rest of my mission and returned home to tell my story. No one had broken any flight regulations. We'd each had a lesson reinforced: Keep your head out of the cockpit.

I remember another flight at Hurlburt Field just as clearly. Sometimes we'd fly with one instructor for only a flight or two and then switch. One day I was assigned Captain Moore. Captain Moore was old enough to be a colonel. There were rumors that he'd been demoted for some unspecified bad incident or incidents. He seemed like a ne'er-do-well—loose, undisciplined, too talkative. During the preflight briefing he explained that he was going to show me how to find specific geographic spots on the ground very quickly. "Edgerton," he finally said, "I'm going to teach you navigation—dead reckoning—like you've never been taught before. All you need is a compass, a watch, and a map. The compass is in the aircraft, the watch is on your wrist, and here's the map. Let's go fly."

We arrived in the practice area. Captain Moore talked me through (1) determining wind direction, (2) confirming wind direction by flying from one known point to another, (3) calculating speed, distance, and time, (4) properly flying over a starting point, and (5) finding the destination point with a watch. He demonstrated the use of section lines on a map to help me simplify dead reckoning. After a short demonstration of a part of the lesson, he'd give me control of the aircraft and ask me to accomplish the procedure he'd just demonstrated. Then he'd explain more, give me control, and ask me to perform again, and so on.

Finally, in about an hour, I was a master of dead reckoning. I had never flown a better-instructed flight. Nor would I.

AT THE END of our OV-10 training, we turned in our choices for our next assignment. I asked to fly over Laos rather than South Vietnam. After each mission I'd be able to return to a comfortable base. I wouldn't chance living in a tent. Maybe it was more risky than flying over Vietnam, but maybe not.

I was given my first choice: I'd be flying out of Nakhon Phanom Air Base in northeast Thailand. I vaguely remember my romantic notions about it all. My earlier letter to my father was a clear statement of my beliefs about why I was going into the war: I was part of a military arm of my nation and I was acting to prevent enemy troops from landing on the shores of America and taking over my country. I was needed. Besides all that, and maybe mostly, I wanted to fly the OV-10 in combat. I wanted the adventure. I wanted to see myself doing something like that.

On to Southeast Asia

BEFORE GOING TO THAILAND, I took a six-week survival course in the Philippines. Unlike the general survival course at Fairchild Air Force Base, this course was specifically geared to the jungle. A new group of pilots and I sat through classes on evasion techniques and spent time in the jungle. We were shown plants to eat and plants to leave alone; in fact we were given a deck of cards with photographs of jungle plants, labeled.

I met Dan "Hoot" Gibson, a dry-witted captain my age. Hoot was a career officer, but he had an informality about him that I liked. We shared a kind of unconscious distance from what we were doing, a distance that allowed room for humor. I couldn't have said why I liked him back then, nor could I have said that about Johnny Hobbs or Jim Butts, or other good friends in Yokota, but looking back, I see that our shared distance somehow supported our friendship. We weren't as serious—in a gung ho, careerist way—as many other pilots.

FROM THE PHILIPPINES we were flown to Cam Ranh Bay, South Vietnam, for "orientation" to Southeast Asia. I remember walking off the cargo plane. I sensed a voice saying, You are here. You are in Vietnam. This is it. You are here.

I was silent, overwhelmed, alone, looking over a tall chain-link fence bordering the airfield at surrounding mountains pockmarked with bomb craters. I sensed that "the enemy" was out there somewhere, brooding, waiting for my blood. I was afraid, but I felt safe, somehow confident that bad stuff would happen to the other guy.

Part of our several days of orientation was a course on maintaining good relations with local populations. I saved one of the handouts:

DOS AND DON'TS FOR AMERICANS IN SOUTHEAST ASIA

1. Do not make unfavorable comparisons between the way things are done in the U.S. and Vietnam.

2. Do show interest in history and culture of Vietnam to include religion, folklore and holidays.

3. Do avoid controversial subjects in conversation. Personal views are taken as those of your employer or government.

4. Do be modest about your possessions.

5. Do accept courtesy and respect with dignity.

6. Do be patient. A Vietnamese behaves very reasonably by his own standards.

7. Do be quiet and dignified at all times. Any loud or exaggerated behavior is considered vulgar, especially in public.

8. Do maintain self-control at all times. Do not get upset or show temper if things go badly.

9. Do laugh heartily at comic actions or dragon dancers when laughter is praise.

10. Do not boast about physical prowess. Vietnamese associate strength with lowest classes of their own society and make a virtue of avoiding physical exertion. They are sensitive about their small and slender physique. They resent anything which could be interpreted as a challenge.

11. Do not laugh at a Vietnamese or put him in a position to be laughed at by others. This causes him to lose face—a very serious matter to Chinese and Vietnamese.

12. Do not ridicule a student if you are the teacher.

13. Do keep hands off people's heads, particularly children's heads. The head is the most sacred part of the body.

14. Do not be offended if a Vietnamese man holds your hand. For Vietnamese this signifies nothing other than friendship and should be interpreted as a compliment.

15. Do not put your feet on a table, desk or chair.

I never considered the tone of the handout. I just read it and put it away.

I remember the beach at Cam Ranh: a U-shaped bay of white sand up against low, steep green mountains. I remember thinking it was one of the most beautiful beaches I'd ever seen.

PART 5

(1970–71)

COMBAT

Nakhon Phanom

NAKHON PHANOM AIR BASE in Thailand was about what I'd expected. Some buildings seemed hastily constructed. The flight line area, where airplanes were kept, had a kind of steel netting on the ground rather than asphalt. The netting covered taxiways and places for the airplanes to sit while not flying; the runways were paved.

I lived in a room in a long, narrow building with identical rooms side by side—a kind of very long, one-story motel on low pilings. A narrow boardwalk extended the length of the building, and across a grassy area sat another building, identical to ours. In the grassy area sat the Nailhole, our thatched-roof bar.

There were two groups of fliers in our squadron: the night fliers, who flew 0-2s (small push-pull propeller aircraft) and the day fliers, who flew OV-10s. My roommate was a tall, thin, redheaded night flier from South Carolina, Rick Sizemore. Within a few days of my arrival we hung a dark, heavy cloth curtain across the middle of our room so that the window and door, along with my bed, desk, and chair, were on my side. He'd sleep most of the day on his side, where he also had a desk and chair as well as his bed, and while he flew at night, I'd sleep. On my desk were envelopes, writing paper, a journal, good-luck charms, a portable cassette tape recorder for messages to and from home, my Super-8 camera, and sometimes cigarettes.

Hoot Gibson, whom I'd met in the Philippines, ended up at Nakhon Phanom also. On the first night of the day that he and I and a few other new pilots arrived in Nakhon Phanom (NKP), a welcoming party was held in the Nailhole. The hut housed one large room with a Ping-Pong table, dart boards, and the bar, run by a Thai bartender, Paul—surely not his real name.

Initiation into our squadron, the Twenty-third Tactical Air Support Squadron (TASS), called for us to chug a glass of green liquid called a hammer and then say why we were happy to be a Nail (our call sign. I was assigned Nail 38). The hammer was about six ounces of vodka with a touch of green food coloring.

Lots of laughing and cheering.

On that night, as the party began to wind down, someone suggested a game of blow hockey.

"Too late for that," said a pilot. "I'm going to bed."

There was some murmuring. Then a pilot named Scott said, "Okay, I'll play. How about you, Edgerton? Game of blow hockey?"

"Sure." This was not a time for backing down. (As I look back, I see there never was.)

A rectangular lunch tray with the rough markings of a

hockey field was placed on a small table and filled to the brim with water.

A short, stocky pilot said, "Okay, I'm the referee. Who else is playing?"

"I am," said Scott. He pulled a chair up to his end of the tray. Someone put a chair down for me, and I sat.

"I got five dollars on Scott," I heard.

"Ten on Edgerton."

Money was changing hands. Someone patted me on the back. "Go get him, Edge."

"Okay," said the referee, standing between us. Then he chanted, "Positions, men. Chins on the table, hands behind your back. Blow the target into the opponent's goal. Three out of five wins. No movement beyond the edge of the tray. On three. One, two, *three*." He dropped a cork in the middle of the hockey field, and we began blowing the cork in opposite directions. Before I could get my bearings, the cork was in my goal. The referee picked it up. Cheering all around. "Positions, men. On three. One, two, *three*." This time I managed to score a goal. More cheering, some booing.

The referee picked up the cork. "Positions, men." Two more goals and I'd win. I had to get this one. "One, two"— as the referee brought his hand down to drop the cork, it continued downward, but toward me—"*three*." My face and head were soaked in water. A great cheer erupted, and pilots began slapping me on the back and welcoming me into the fraternity of Nail FACs. Someone had earlier escorted Hoot and the other new recruits outside. We would get them one at a time over the next few nights.

Laughing and cheering were not uncommon in the Nailhole, a building with one purpose: to provide relief from war. We spent a lot of time there, and if not there, then in the squadron building near the flight line, getting ready to fly, or in the officer's club dining room or bar.

New pilots were assigned flying instructors. I was assigned Captain Don Charles. His job was to get me re-acclimated to the OV-10 by flying aerobatics, instrument approaches, and simulated single-engine landings. I'd also fly after dark to "safe" areas in western Laos, where I'd practice dropping flares and shooting smoke rockets. The flares, after release, would be suspended from a slowly falling parachute and would show the ground beneath as if it were one very large, lit football field. Later missions would call for flying after dusk, or before dawn.

Then I had to fly several combat missions with Captain Charles before being turned loose on my own. I remember our first. We briefed for the flight and then caught a van from the squadron building over to headquarters. We were checked into that building by a guard, who read from the badges hanging around our necks. Inside, we found several other pilots in a small briefing room. I was surprised when a woman entered, Lieutenant Erickson — the intelligence officer. Before briefing us, she introduced a captain who gave the weather briefing. Low clouds were a problem that day. An ideal day for a FAC who wanted to fly was clear weather. If the ground was overcast below our minimum flying altitude, we didn't fly. Broken clouds presented problems because they often drifted over a target area.

Then Lieutenant Erickson used a pointer to indicate "safe areas," areas suitable for bailout, on a large map of Laos. She also pointed out areas of heavy triple-A firings (antiaircraft artillery) on previous days. As FACs we'd need to pass this information along (in a short prestrike briefing) to the fighter-bombers we'd direct on air strikes.

And then she said, "There's a large concentration of gomers [enemy troops] just to the south of Delta Three Three [a point on the map]." She would be briefing most days for months to come, and she used the word *gomers* as casually as she would the word *pencil*. We would use it too.

We flew reconnaissance that day, looking for trucks, but found none. Troops were rarely seen. They were protected by jungle foliage. We were scheduled to direct bombers to cut a road. Captain Charles pointed out landmarks and helped me find our target, and when the fighters arrived, he assisted me in directing them to cut the road. He made all radio calls, simplifying my job, and I did all the flying. Much of the time I was confused or lost, and I was continually trying to update my position by matching ground features to map features. Because of the interference of low clouds, the bombers had problems with accuracy. No bombs hit the road. I watched for ground fire, but I didn't see any. I knew that the most common antiaircraft artillery was thirty-seven-millimeter guns. I'd been told that their tracers, coming every few rounds, looked like orange Coke bottles streaking up from the ground.

After the bombers left to return to their base in Vietnam and we reported by radio to a command center that there was no damage to the road, I flew around looking for trucks and familiarizing myself with the general area below me. Any combat mission was flown in a numbered "sector" about a hundred miles square, and that particular area was the responsibility of a single FAC. We looked for trucks or any other signs of life in our sector, and we directed all air strikes. No other FAC would be flying in our area while we were there, nor would any U.S. military aircraft fly through a sector without our clearance.

We'd been told over and over that while flying above Laos we always had to "jink" to the left or right at different degrees of bank. This way, enemy gunners would have difficulty getting a "bead" on us. We knew to jink every second that we were flying over Laos.

At some point along toward the end of this, my first mission, I became engrossed with cockpit duties, including studying the maps in my lap, and I stopped jinking for several seconds. Suddenly I felt a jolt and heard a pop directly underneath the aircraft.

From the backseat: "Good God, man. *Jink.* They're shooting at us."

Fired at already! I pulled the aircraft into a left bank and then a quick right bank. Back to the left. I looked below but could see nothing except stretches of green jungle and long, steep, rocky east-west rises we called karst.

We flew home and landed. I had an idea what I'd be doing for the next year or so.

One day a few weeks after that first combat ride, Captain Charles and I were having a drink at the Nailhole, and he said, "Do you remember that first flight, when we got fired at?"

"Yep."

"That was me banging my feet on the floor in the backseat. But don't spread the word. Surprise is the key. I got the shit scared out of me the same way."

I finished my checkout and started flying solo combat missions. Typically a target would be a section of the Ho Chi Minh Trail, the north-south, trans-Laos network of dirt roads through the jungle. We would direct fighter-bombers to bomb the trail, leaving a crater that couldn't be crossed by a truck. Before takeoff we would be given "line numbers" for prearranged targets (used so that coordinates would not need to be read over the radio and possibly picked up by enemy monitors). Sometimes a target would be a suspected storage area or a river ford, and we would be given the time for rendezvous with the fighter-bombers.

We used an encoder/decoder "wheel" (it had fresh numbers every day) to encode numbers that needed to be recited over the airwaves. We always carried grease marker pens and used them to write radio frequencies, bomb-damage assessments, and so forth on our Plexiglas canopies in the lower left or right front corners. I got the hang of things quickly and started feeling at home in my job.

Occasionally we would see a parked truck or what might be a storage facility under the jungle canopy—a target that had not been scheduled for bombing. In that case we'd call King, the airborne command center, and they would send fighter-bombers, if available, from a carrier in the Gulf of Tonkin or from an air base in Vietnam or Thailand, or from another mission that had not required them to drop all their bombs.

During all my flying over Laos, I do not recall seeing one standing building or obviously inhabited area. The Ho Chi Minh Trail, where people had once lived, was deserted except for those bringing supplies from North Vietnam through Laos and into South Vietnam or providing shelter or operating the large antiaircraft guns hidden along the trail.

There were four "boxes" in southern Laos. These boxes, several miles square, where trails intersected or had once intersected, were targets when aircraft over Laos carried bombs but had nowhere to drop them. The boxes had been bombed until not one tree stood. They looked like the surface of the moon—nothing but sand and bomb craters. And on some mornings, through binoculars, I'd see truck tracks around craters and across a box.

B-52 bombers flew "arc light" missions. Suspected concentrations of enemy troops, trucks, or supplies would be bombed with hundreds of five-hundred-pound bombs (from one B-52). When an arc light was scheduled for my sector, I stayed clear of the area and watched a B-52 fly over far above, leaving contrails, and then in the jungle far down below, an area about the size of a town would suddenly explode beneath the jungle canopy.

If we saw a convoy of trucks moving (I never saw trucks moving at any time other than dawn or dusk), we were to dive immediately and fire a rocket. When a smoke rocket exploded near a truck convoy, the truck drivers usually assumed an air strike was coming and quickly parked and deserted their trucks, climbing into "spider holes" (small bunkers). Otherwise, when resting or stopping, they hid their trucks under thick jungle foliage.

EARLY IN MY TOUR, I had the opportunity to visit a top secret facility on base. Inside, a map with electric lighting behind it covered an entire wall. The sergeant leading the tour explained that certain markings on the map indicated where U.S. Air Force jet fighters had dropped sensitive hearing devices along the Ho Chi Minh Trail. The devices were located in small green plastic trees—at their base, where the trees planted themselves into the ground. The sounds of passing trucks on the trail could be heard in this room in Thailand. Specialists could hear voices, men around campfires occasionally, once arguing about Marlboro cigarettes. Most important, when trucks were heard moving along the trail (usually at night), jets could be summoned to drop bombs on the trail near the hearing devices.

The electronic wall confirmed our technical superiority over the enemy. And what an incredible technological advantage we had. We controlled the skies over Laos. We could bomb at will. How could they win?

Instructing in War

AFTER ABOUT SIX WEEKS of flying solo combat missions, I became an instructor. I still flew solo missions, but I also instructed the new guys arriving from the States. And on every pilot's first combat mission, as soon as he flew straight and level for a few seconds, I lifted my feet in the backseat and crashed them to the floor. "Whoa! Jink, man! They're shooting at us!"

As new pilots arrived, old pilots left. At a going-away party in the Nailhole soon after I arrived, a departing pilot proposed a toast to the truck drivers on the trail, our enemy. I was surprised, but none of the old-timers seemed to be. There was a respect for the resilience of those forces on the ground in Laos. This toast, it turned out, was not uncommon.

After a month or so of combat flying over the trail, I'd still not seen any antiaircraft fire. But some was coming right up.

My first trainee was Harley Williams, a young pilot just

out of pilot training. Harley was relatively slow but so sincere and good humored you couldn't help liking him.

We had the early flight—one that would put us over the Ho Chi Minh Trail at between 6:00 and 6:30 a.m. just as the night FAC would be departing our sector. We briefed at 3:30 a.m., carefully going over all aspects of the flight. I quizzed him on emergency procedures. The bold-faced items in emergency procedures from our checklist had to be memorized. The other items would be read aloud.

ENGINE FIRE DURING FLIGHT

1. **AFFECTED ENGINE CONDITION LEVER—FEATHER & FUEL SHUT-OFF.**
2. **FIRE LIGHT—PULL.**
3. **FIRE EXT—AGENT.**
4. If still on fire—**EJECT OR LAND IMMEDIATELY.**
5. Failed engine **FUEL EMERG SHUTOFF—SHUT-OFF.**

We caught a van and rode to headquarters for a pre-flight briefing (intelligence and weather) lasting from 4:20 to about 4:50. Then we rode a van to the flight line, found our airplane, and had about thirty minutes for a thorough preflight check. I hadn't thought about giving Harley extra time.

At 5:15 a.m. we were in the aircraft ready to crank. After flying the OV-10 most days for six weeks, as Harley had been doing (pilots on their first flying assignments had an extended checkout period), a cockpit check (forty-one items) and engine start (about fifteen items) could normally be finished in less than five minutes. A pilot reading checklist items aloud and performing tasks sounded like this: "Gust lock, removed. Thruster safety pin, removed. Survival kit, attached. Riser attach fittings, secured . . ."

But for Williams it was, "Gust lock, removed." One thousand one, one thousand two, one thousand three, one thousand four. "Thruster safety pin, removed." One thousand one, one thousand two, one thousand three, one thousand four, one thousand five, one thousand six. "Survival kit, attached." One thousand one, one thousand two . . .

But I knew it would be wrong to hurry him at this point in his training. We'd be a few minutes late for takeoff, but we could add a few knots to our cruise speed and make it to our area on time.

I instructed Harley to identify himself as "in training" when he first talked to the fighters: "Copper Lead, this is Nail Two Two in training." That way the fighter pilots would know an instructor was flying in the backseat.

The first strike seemed routine at the outset—it was to cut the trail—except that Harley, as usual, was a bit slow. But not so slow that I had to take over. Our mics, on the ends of thin rods extending from our helmets, were hot, meaning we could talk to each other without holding down the mic button on the throttle grip. (Oxygen masks weren't needed in the OV-10 because we never flew above twelve thousand feet, the minimum altitude for oxygen.) To talk to the fighters, however, he or I would press the mic button under our left thumb.

I was helping Harley decide where to orbit while the fighters put in their ordnance.

"Did you see that at three o'clock?" he said.

"What?"

"I don't know, unless it's triple-A."

There, at our three o'clock position, were ghastly small white puffs of smoke—from flak. And back behind us too. And down there below, those orange Coke bottles, seeming to start not in the jungle but just above it, streaking up one after the other.

"Keep jinking," I said. I was astonished. The whole world had changed. What I had been hearing about for weeks was happening. Now. And I was in it. In this sudden, new, surreal world, all laws stopped, all courtesies had succumbed to something dark, sad, depressed, hell-bent for grim death. In this sudden world were no manners, no nods of goodwill, no indifference even. Indifference had been sucked from the world, and in its place somebody in the present time, in this living instant from the ground below, was trying to kill me, and I was sitting high, high in the air . . .

With Harley.

But wasn't there a bubble of protection around the airplane? Wasn't there a bubble of . . . they wouldn't hit us, would they? Didn't I also have a protective shield of some sort around my body, an outline of invisible light that was created by the love of my father and mother, my aunts and uncles, by the home grass and dirt in the yards of the one white frame and the one brick home I knew from my childhood? Wouldn't I be protected somehow by the love and care of all my elementary school teachers—Mrs. Monday, my first-grade teacher, and Mrs. Arants and

Mrs. Tilly, my second- and third-grade teachers, those women who ruled and taught and protected?

"I have the aircraft," I said. I wanted to be flying. I turned the aircraft abruptly so that I could see below, see clearly where the fire might be coming from. We were supposed to turn toward rather than away from ground fire in hopes that the gunners would fear we'd spotted them. It didn't always work; the guns, so well camouflaged, were difficult to spot, even through binoculars.

I pressed the mic button, pushing the throttle forward. I needed more power to maneuver. "Copper Flight," I said. My spirit was above somewhere, watching my body follow procedures, not cut and run. My mind was somewhere between my spirit and my body, holding on, remembering training, remembering drill and practice. "Nail Two Two. We're receiving triple-A. Copper Two, you're cleared in. Safe areas north and northwest." I tried to sound normal. A main element of our job was to be in control, calm, re-assuring. If someone were shot down—and bailed out and parachuted into the jungle—my job would be to talk to him by radio, to reassure him, to remind him to pull in his chute so that it would not be easily seen by enemy troops, to remind him to hide carefully, to move slowly in order to conserve energy, to get him to preserve radio batteries, to indicate enemy troop positions. The search and rescue team (called a SAR)—two World War II A-1E fighters and an HH-53 Jolly Green Giant helicopter—was forty-five minutes away at Nakhon Phanom.

No aircraft was hit by triple-A that day, and we returned home safely. My time as a SAR coordinator would come later, after triple-A fire had become more routine.

EACH EVENING, THE next day's flight schedule was posted on a bulletin board in the Nailhole. I was elated when scheduled to fly solo, about one in three of my flights. If I were flying those missions today, I'd be tentative and more afraid. In my recurring dreams of combat flying, I spend time on the flight line looking for my aircraft, and if I find it, I taxi out, only to find there's an unknown mechanical problem preventing takeoff. Sometimes I become bogged down trying to solve a mathematical problem I've never seen before.

But back then, besides lacking a perspective that allowed for the possibility of my own death, my knowledge of procedures and of my airplane was so thorough and practiced that I impressed myself with what I could do, and I knew that when I met up with a flight of fighter-bombers over Laos I would be professional and exact. Though I'd been shot at and felt a slice of emotion I'd never experienced before, I still felt invincible, and I'm sure most other pilots felt the same way.

On these solo FAC missions, I'd often enjoy the extreme solitude that I've found only in an airplane. The quiet times flying to and from my sector were almost otherworldly. Tall, billowing clouds, nearby or far away, seemed to offer safety and comfort. Underneath the confidence that I'd survive was a small voice warning of the danger on some future mission, but not this one, and the thirty-minute trips out and back were bookends of refuge.

But the exhilaration I felt over Laos came from more than being alone in an airplane—it was somehow related to my tasks over Laos, the use of skills learned to keep myself alive. I knew the limits of my aircraft and its systems, and I was confident performing my tasks.

After sighting triple-A fire that first time, sightings came regularly.

One day, City Flight, two single-seat A-7s, Navy fighter-bombers, had arrived over a highly defended intersection of trails. Number two was pulling up out of his bomb pass when I saw the flak around him—white puffs of smoke in the air. The pattern of flak suggested twenty-three-millimeter-gun fire, very dangerous at lower altitudes. Suddenly a stream of white smoke, perhaps fuel, streaked out behind City 2's left wing. Over the radio came, "Nail, this is City Two. I'm hit."

"Roger, City Two, you're trailing smoke." My voice was too high. I tried to relax my vocal cords. "Head one two zero degrees. There are safe areas all along your route." I got my voice back down. "Your nearest base is Da Nang. Stand by for the numbers [radio frequencies for Da Nang]." I looked them up and then gave him the radio and navigational frequencies he needed.

After I landed, I called Da Nang by landline. City 2 had landed safely.

ONE DAY WHILE being fired at I felt a sudden thud somewhere in the aircraft and thought I'd been hit. All controls and warning lights were normal, but I knew not to take chances. I headed for NKP and declared an emergency so that the fire trucks would be waiting in case aircraft damage caused landing problems. After landing, maintenance personnel found no sign of damage.

On another occasion, within a few minutes of takeoff my instruments indicated a fire in the right engine. I immediately shut it down, flew back to the base, and landed from a spiraling-down approach used for single-engine landings. No sign of fire was found.

The OV-10 flew nicely on just one engine, but precautions were necessary. It was not unusual at the end of a training mission, while the trainee was flying up front, for me to pull one of the throttles to idle and say, "We're simulating a lost engine. What do you do?" The student would then recite the part of the emergency procedure that he'd memorized (boldfaced print) and then read the rest.

1. **FAILED ENGINE CONDITION LEVER — FEATHER & FUEL SHUT-OFF.**
2. Operative engine power lever — **ADVANCE**, as required.
3. Gear — **UP**.
4. Flaps — **UP**.
5. Maintain minimum single-engine speed or above.
6. Stores — **JETTISON**, as required.
7. Attempt air starts.
8. Failed engine power lever — **FLIGHT IDLE**.
9. Failed engine **FUEL EMERG SHUTOFF — SHUT OFF**.

But the student pilot would not actually feather or shut off fuel to the engine. An idling engine and a feathered engine (which means that the propeller blades are stopped and locked with their flat surfaces turned parallel to the wind flow in order to reduce drag) have similar effects on overall drag. After reciting the entire procedure, he'd fly back to base and land with one operating engine and one idling engine.

Flying on one engine, the twin-engine OV-10 was lethargic. If it got too slow, a stall was likely, therefore the spiraling-down approach mentioned above was used when landing with only one engine. Instead of approaching the airfield at fifteen hundred feet above the ground, the pilot approached at above twenty-five hundred feet and spiraled down, hitting certain key altitudes so that gravity rather than engine power helped control the approach to landing. Single-engine landings were practiced often, ideally without advancing either throttle beyond idle, thus simulating a double-engine failure.

Another Letter Home

A BUDDY, MIKE AIKEN, Nail 18, flying near the North Vietnamese border, was jumped and shot at by a couple of North Vietnamese fighter jets. This was unusual. An audio-cassette of radio transmissions during the flight became available and I sent it to my father. At the same time, I sent voice recordings from a failed prison raid near Hanoi. All but the bracketed information below was in the letter sent with the tapes.

> Daddy, here are 2 [audio]tapes—the first one is of Nail 18 (that's his call sign) getting chased and shot at by two North Vietnam jet fighters (MIGs). I'll try to explain and you can refer to this letter as you listen.
>
> Bandits—this means enemy fighters.
>
> Cricket—is the call sign of the U.S. controlling people.
>
> King—the people who control rescue efforts if they are needed.

The Barrel refers to a large section of northern Laos known as the Barrel Roll.

Nail 18 says, "Cricket, this is Nail 18. I just got a tallyho [means "I just saw"] on one of the MIGs up here—he just made a pass on me. I'm taking fire too, Cricket."

Somebody calls about two blue bandits (MIGs) attacking (these people had picked the MIGs up on radar). Right after this, Nail 18 says he had a couple of MIG-21s and "you might want to advise the boys" (the rescue people).

Nail 18 says, "One just made another pass on me— they're still up here hosing" (shooting).

Raven 27 (a U.S. pilot) [on a top secret mission . . . these were "forest rangers" stationed in northern Laos] calls and gives his position.

Nail 18 says, "Got one in sight. He's still circling me. Tallyho on the other one. They're both down here now. He's coming in on another pass now."

Cricket says, "We've got a Falcon Flight outbound to you" (this is a flight of two U.S. fighters).

Nail 18: "I've got them on both sides of me now."

Nail 18 heads "due south" for the "high terrain" [mountains].

Nail 18 says he "got rid of all his stores" (means he jettisoned his external fuel tank and rocket containers, etc.) and then says he's going to RTB (return to base— NKP—because of low fuel).

Cricket says, "They're back over toward the Fish's Mouth, so stay low" (he means the MIGs are still in the area—somebody picked them up on radar).

Soon afterward this guy who just happens to be in

the area calls—this is funny—and asks about the warning.

Then Cricket says, "They're chasing Nail 18 up there."

The guy comes back, "I'll be go to hell."

The last thing Nail 18 says is "apparently about the only damage I got here is the mess in the cockpit."

(Nail 18 is Lt. Mike Aiken—a good friend of mine.)

[I explained in the letter that Mike came home and landed safely. The tape that I sent of radio transmissions from the prison raid near Hanoi was of the now-famous (among historians of the Vietnam War) Son Tay raid. On the morning of the raid, in November 1970, I was scheduled to fly a solo combat mission. After my preflight check I called tower for a clearance to taxi. I was refused clearance, and I knew something was up. I left the aircraft and went inside. Nobody was flying and nobody knew why. Later we discovered that the prison raid had been taking place near Hanoi, and for security reasons, nobody was flying over Laos.]

OK, Daddy, this next one is of the prison raid and it's very confusing. I'll get good information on it later but right now you'll have to do with what I can give you. Here are the important call signs:

<u>Wildroot</u>—the people in a helicopter who were controlling the whole thing.

<u>Axle</u>—people who landed outside the prison camp, I think, one of them landing in the wrong place, as you can tell.

<u>Greenleaf</u>—these are the people who crash-landed a helicopter in the camp and searched it to rescue the

prisoners. When they say "negative items," that means they found no prisoners. Later you hear the code word NILE RICE, which meant "unsuccessful."

Blueboy—people inside the camp also. They talk about "blowing the wall."

Peach—this was the call sign of the American propeller-driven fighter aircraft. They talk about "taking care of the bridge" and "strafe from the west."

Later you hear Blueboy and Redwine loading up into the helicopters after they find no prisoners.

A little later you hear "SAM, SAM, SAM." These are the pilots as they see surface-to-air missiles being fired at them.

Later you hear one pilot telling another pilot to "go down—lower. Get down on the deck. Turn left." This pilot is trying to direct the other pilot away from a missile.

That's about it. Hope you enjoyed them.

[There was an addendum to the letter.]

Daddy, I found out who the people are on the prison raid; here goes:

Peach 1, 2, 3, 4, 5—A-1E propeller-driven fighter aircraft.

Apple 1, 2, 3, 4, 5—helicopters.

Apple 5—helicopter that landed in the prison yard. The team that was on this helicopter had the call sign of Blueboy. The helicopter cut its engine and glided into the compound and crash-landed. This was so the motor could not be heard as they approached and thus give away their position.

Axle—a ground unit that was placed in the wrong place by Apple 1. Apple 1 did not come back to pick the men up, but Apple 2 did. The commander of the Axle team, called Axle 1, ran from the wrong spot, where they were put down, to the right spot. The job of the Axle team was to cut off part of the prison from the outside.

Wildroot—the ground commander.

Greensleaves—a group that set up a defensive position at a bridge nearby.

Fruit Salad—what Wildroot said when he was talking to everybody.

Gearbox—the Air Force commander who was in South Vietnam.

I can see my father sitting on his side of the couch in front of the fireplace, leaning back, his spectacles reflecting light from the overheard fixture in the little sitting room off the kitchen. In the letter, I said I hoped he enjoyed the tape. I wanted to share the thrill with someone in my family, and he was the one I chose. For me, this was all thrill, adventure, pure, simple. I doubt that he, in any sense, enjoyed what he heard.

Bangkok and Prairie Fire

AFTER SIX WEEKS of flying duty, a pilot was given four days of vacation. It was called combat time off or CTO. Normally, for our four-day break, we'd catch a cargo plane (usually a C-130) with empty space for a ride into Bangkok and then catch a cab to the Americana Hotel.

Sometimes we'd need to wait a day, or even two, for a cargo plane with space. But my friend Hoot, now flying with Prairie Fire, code name for a top secret mission, had connections with the Army, and one day he handed me a set of "Blanket Travel/Classified Courier Orders, 18 Feb 1971," made out for the two of us, saying that he and I should receive preference for a ride in any U.S. cargo plane at any time, and that we could wear civilian clothes and carry a weapon. With the new set of orders, there was no more waiting for rides to Bangkok, though we never carried anything other than the orders themselves.

In Bangkok, our regular cab driver was John, a Thai man who became our tour guide and friend. He'd drive us around for several days, never asking for money. After taking us to the airport for our return trip, he'd stand before us, lift the flap to his upper shirt pocket, and look the other way. We'd insert his pay, much more than if he'd charged his normal fee.

We'd heard about a beach with white sands in southern Thailand, a place called Pattaya Beach. Hoot and I headed that way during one of our CTOs. When we arrived at midday, rain was pouring, and it continued into the second day. No beach time. On that second afternoon we found a local bar. We sat at a booth, and in the wall at the end of our table was a large aquarium. We kept trekking to the door to see if the rain had finally stopped. Each time, it hadn't. In the aquarium, which looked almost like a window to the outside, four or five large fish faced us. They seemed lazy, drugged. Their mouths opened and closed, opened and closed.

After a sip of beer, Hoot, straight faced, looked at the fish and then at me and, nodding his head toward the fish, said, "This rain is getting ridiculous."

I glanced at the fish, and what Hoot had said wasn't especially funny. But then I glanced at them again, imagining I was looking outside through a window. There were those lazy fish sitting there, having just swum up to our window in the flood, mouths opening and closing, opening and closing. I laughed. We changed the subject. I looked back at the fish. Now it was really funny, and finally it was so funny that I was lying in the booth, laughing. Soon it was funny to Hoot, too.

I recently tracked Hoot down, called him on the phone.

We had not seen or heard from each other in thirty-three years. We exchanged greetings, and he said, "Hey, do you remember that afternoon we were—"

"The fish," I said.

It was still funny.

Hoot and I liked to dogfight in the OV-10. We'd both been F-4 backseaters and knew air-to-air moves and countermoves. Whenever he and I were scheduled to be in the air at the same time over Laos, we'd be on the watch for each other flying to or from our sectors. One would make erroneous position calls to headquarters to throw the other off. Several times we were in serious dogfights over enemy territory, against regulations.

One day something happened that I never intended to tell anyone. As we were dogfighting, I managed to get behind Hoot. He was in a tight turn. I was pulling g's, staying with him, very excited. I called "Fox Three" over a radio channel I knew he was monitoring. I was so into the action that I instinctively pressed the rocket launch button on the stick grip. But of course my arm switch wasn't turned on. But oh, yes, it was! *Ka-swish*. The sound was sickening. I just missed him. To the rear. (I didn't have enough lead on him.) Had I connected, he may well have been shot out of the air.

He never saw the rocket whiz behind him.

In May of 2004, after contacting Hoot by phone, I saw him for the first time since 1971. We had lunch. Surely after all this time he'd forgive me, maybe even see a little humor in the incident. We reminisced and laughed about the fish in the aquarium again, we told old stories, and when dessert came, I braced myself. "Hoot, I've got to tell you something I've been keeping secret for thirty-three years."

He raised an eyebrow, smiled. "You already told me."

"What? When?"

"The night before you left Thailand you'd had a bit to drink. You pulled me aside and said, 'Hoot, I've got to tell you something that's a big load on me.' Then you told me about shooting the rocket while we were dogfighting."

"Have you told anybody?"

"No."

"Why?"

Hoot looked left, then right, and without cracking a smile said, "Because you got to my six o'clock. Somehow."

PRAIRIE FIRE WAS A highly secret reconnaissance and "deep strike" Army unit based at Nakhon Phanom. Several of our OV-10 pilots flew cover (protection) for them. Hoot was their head pilot. He and a few other pilots used the Nail call sign and were on the books as Nail pilots, but the Prairie Fire mission was different and highly classified. A Prairie Fire mission worked something like this: A small group of soldiers were dropped into Laos at night by helicopter to collect intelligence and harass North Vietnamese and Laotian forces. The FAC's job would be to fly cover—to protect them from the air as they were dropped in or taken out, or if they got into trouble. In some cases the FAC initiated an air strike a few miles from the drop point as a diversionary tactic. The Prairie Fire FAC's OV-10 would be equipped with high-explosive rockets as well as target-marking smoke rockets, and besides directing air strikes, a Prairie Fire pilot could be called upon to strike enemy forces with rockets and with the four machine guns mounted in sponsons on the OV-10. This would happen as low as treetop level or lower. Our forty-five-hundred-foot minimum altitude rule was waived for Prairie Fire pilots.

One night Hoot invited me to a party at the Prairie Fire operations shack, located in a secluded corner of the base. The Prairie Fire Army guys had a reputation for being wild people. I'd heard that on occasion they sometimes ate the legs off live rats, one of their more sedate pastimes.

The party was relatively tame; several guys ate some roses with their champagne and broke champagne bottles against a wall. I came home early because I had to fly the next day. Hoot knocked on my door several hours later. I let him in. He was a bit unsteady. He pulled a mini hand grenade from one of the many pockets on his flight suit. Then he reached into another pocket and pulled out another one.

"I'm going to put these in my survival vest." His speech was slurred.

I looked at one of the grenade pins, the kind with a ring in the end. "You're going to blow your ass off before you ever see a survival vest," I said.

"Oh," he said. "Here's another one."

When he finished pulling grenades from his flight suit, there were thirteen around the room on various surfaces.

He offered me several and I turned him down. He later taped up two for his survival vest so they wouldn't go off accidentally. He told me he had so much tape on them that if he met up with the enemy in Laos, he would have to hold up his hand and ask for a time-out to get the tape off.

The Speaker on the Wall

In early spring 1971 I was flying a routine combat training mission with First Lieutenant Greg Rawlings, Nail 23, fresh from the States. He received a call.

"Nail Two Three, this is Jingo, flight of two F-Fours seeking to enter your sector at Checkpoint Delta and precede northwest for Daisy Bread."

"Roger, Jingo, Nail Two Three, in training, permission granted."

The two F-4s, each with two pilots, would be far below us, streaking into our sector at less than five hundred feet above the ground. Their speed would put them past heavy antiaircraft artillery before gunners knew they were coming. Or at least that was the idea. Their job was to drop those treelike audiorecording sensors near the trail.

I knew our sector was clear, so we could go about our business and avoid putting in any strikes near Jingo's drop area for the next short while.

Within minutes I heard through my earphones an emergency beeper, a sound something like a frantic siren. The beeper was designed to be set off with a button on a hand-held radio by a pilot on the ground or descending in his parachute. We kept a radio in our survival vests along with flares, a holstered .38 pistol, matches, a compass, and so forth—and in Hoot's case, hand grenades.

Sometimes North Vietnamese troops or Pathet Lao troops on the trail would set off such a radio to draw rescue teams into traps, so we were wary of a beeper heard in isolation—that is, with no other indication that an airman was down. But in this case, within seconds of hearing the beeper, I heard Jingo lead calling to his wingman. "Jingo Two, how do you read? Jingo Two, Jingo Two, what is your location?" There was no response, a silence that, along with the beeper, meant that the dreaded had surely happened.

"I have the aircraft," I said to Greg. I turned in the general direction of Jingo Flight's audio sensor drop.

I called King, the people in charge of search and rescue. "King, this is Nail Two Three. Launch the SAR. We have two pilots down in Sector Nine."

I called Jingo Lead, asked for his exact location.

"I'm about two kilos south of Charlie Box."

"Jingo Lead, do you copy the emergency beeper?"

"Roger."

We both suspected—knew—what had happened.

He continued, "They're probably somewhere along a line running twelve or fifteen kilometers south out of Charlie Box, but I'm not sure."

It would take the search and rescue people—two A-1E

Skyraiders and a Jolly Green Giant helicopter—about forty-five minutes to arrive on scene. There would be a crew in the helicopter to drop into the jungle if necessary after the A-1Es had "sanitized" the area around a pilot.

I figured Jingo Lead was probably near bingo fuel (the number of pounds needed to get home safely) and would not be able to stay around. I pictured the two pilots on the ground in the jungle, hiding as they knew to do.

In less than ten minutes I heard Jingo Lead on the radio talking to Jingo 2-Alpha, the front-seater. Two-Bravo would be the backseater. I heard Jingo 2-Alpha say he thought he'd broken his back. My mind was a swirl of images—the pilot on the ground, wounded—and I felt an emotion that verged on panic. But above the incipient panic, looking down, resting above, was a composure ensured by training, and the need to do what had to be done. Also looking down on me from above was the possibility of shame, riding there, waiting for me to make a mistake, to do anything other than what was expected, expected by my country, my squadron, my friends, my training, my home, my imagination. A kind of unparalleled, ultra peer pressure.

Until search and rescue arrived in about forty-five minutes, I, the FAC, would be in charge of search and rescue. My goal would be to locate the two pilots visually and provide any protection to either or both by shooting machine guns and rockets at any North Vietnamese or Laotian troops trying to capture or kill them. This meant that if need be, I'd have to drop to treetop level or below. By coincidence, for the first time ever, because of a scheduling miscue, I'd been assigned a Prairie Fire aircraft, which was loaded with a pod of seven high-explosive rockets (HEs) along with a pod of smoke rockets.

"We might need those HEs," I said to Greg.

Greg said nothing.

As we arrived near the area of the crash, I saw Jingo Lead's aircraft. He had climbed to an altitude not very high above us.

"Jingo Lead," I said, "this is Nail Two Three. How's your fuel?"

"I'm bingo."

"Roger. I'll take over. The SAR has been launched."

The F-4 raised his wing and headed home.

"Jingo Two-Alpha, Jingo Two-Bravo, this is Nail Two Three. How do you read."

A voice whispered, just loud enough for me to hear clearly, "This is Jingo Two-Alpha. I'm on the ground. I think my back is broken. There are enemy troops nearby."

It was as if I were in a very bad dream.

"Copy. Pull in your parachute, and remain stationary. If you're under good cover, do not move to any other location."

"Roger."

My next job was to find him or Jingo 2-Bravo below. I needed to initiate a series of procedures that the SAR team would continue as soon as they arrived. But a very low cloud cover was over the general area where they'd bailed out—a big, flat white cloud way down there just above the ground. I knew that rows of mountains ran east-west under those clouds. And I knew we were in an area known for heavy antiaircraft artillery. The downed pilots would be very difficult to find, since no one had seen them go in.

"Two-Alpha, can you give me your location?"

"Negative," he whispered. "I'm not sure."

"We're going to get you out. Search and rescue is on the way and I'm coming down to find you. Do you know if Bravo is okay?"

"He bailed out. Yes, I think he's okay."

I called to the backseater, "Jingo Two-Bravo, how do you read? Over."

No response.

"Alpha, can you hear my aircraft above you?"

He whispered, "That's affirmative."

I banked the aircraft and looked far below. The large, flat cloud was covering all the ground below me. I didn't know the altitude of the cloud base—nor of the tallest mountain below, perhaps *in* the clouds.

"Greg, get your map out and tell me the highest elevation in the area below us."

Using distant landmarks, I calibrated my position and then started a spiraling dive toward the flat cloud top. It was easy to see over the student from my high backseat. Our normal minimum altitude, forty-five hundred feet above the ground, was no longer a factor. I was about to descend to treetop level if necessary. Any precautions at all, any acting on fear of being shot at or shot down, was extinguished by those forces above me, watching. Two human beings were counting on me to save their lives. I was their only hope right now. There was only one thing to do:

to go down and try to find them, and when I found them, to try to understand the situation and quickly decide what to do next.

Suddenly, all through me ran a sense of fearlessness. The instinct to protect myself had lifted. Looking back, I see that, operating on some kind of strange, almost mad instinct, I would have died trying to save those guys. I do not see my actions as courageous. Rather, they were the only actions available. Doing anything else would have been more difficult than doing what I was doing.

"Thirty-four hundred feet is what I come up with," said Greg. "That's the top of the highest mountain in the grid below us."

I was approaching the flat cloud top. I looked at my map. I had to see for myself. The elevation of the highest point of land in each map grid was printed on the map in the top right corner of that grid. Yes, the tallest mountain in the grid we were above appeared to be thirty-four hundred feet.

I continued my spiraling dive, making it more shallow.

"We'll either break out below the clouds or we'll start climbing back up at thirty-six hundred feet," I said. The two hundred feet was insurance.

We entered the cloud above four thousand feet, and I kept my eyes glued to my instruments. We were descending slowly in a wide circle. Thirty-eight hundred feet, thirty-seven hundred. I slowly began to level the aircraft.

We were suddenly below the clouds. There under my wings was the jungle.

"Jingo Two-Alpha. Nail Two Three. How do you read?"

No response.

"Jingo Two-Alpha. How do you read? Over."

A mountain stood between us and him. Either that, or troops were so close to him he could not talk. I looked all around, jinking my aircraft madly. I saw nothing but jungle. I climbed back into the clouds. If he was in another valley, he'd never hear my radio at low altitude.

"Nail Two Three, this is Sandy One Two. We're a flight of two plus one. We're proceeding to your area. We're about fifteen minutes out."

"Copy Nail Two Three."

Sandy would be one of the two A-1Es with the Jolly Green Giant helicopter. The A-1Es were used on rescue missions because they were so tough and so difficult to shoot down, as mentioned earlier, in large part because of the relatively simple design of their operational systems. And because they were relatively slow and could turn sharply, there was less time between strikes than with jets. The helicopter was very large and heavily armored.

"Jingo Two-Alpha. Nail Two Three. How do you read? Jingo, Jingo. How do you read?"

Nothing.

We climbed back up through the clouds and got Jingo 2-Alpha on the radio about the time the Sandys arrived. He was whispering again. "I think my back is broken. I have enemy troops all around."

Oh, God, I said to myself. Then I called, "Jingo, this is Nail. We just descended. Did you hear us close to you?"

"Negative."

The Sandys were there. I briefed them on the situation

and turned the rescue mission over to them. The rescue helicopter was waiting several miles away. The plan was that the A-1Es would "neutralize" any resistance to a pickup of the pilot—after he was found—and then the helicopter would pick him up. If necessary, a paramedic would be lowered from the helicopter into the jungle to help the pilot. It's more complicated, but that's the overview.

Sandy called to Jingo, who answered, again whispering. He said he had a bunch of troops around him. I pictured him covered in brush, trying to hide, and I visualized gray-clad North Vietnamese troops—my mind would only handle images of personified evil. This is what the mind allows in a situation like this, and if the mind moves to positions of compromise, negotiation, or consensus, then death is invited, with open arms, into the house.

I had fuel, guns, and rockets and told Sandy Lead that I would hang around if I could be of assistance.

"Nail, we need to fly under the clouds and up some of those valleys down there to try to locate him. Join in as number three. Follow us in extended trail."

Suddenly, AAA flak was going off all around us—a lot of it—apparently being shot into the air blindly from below the clouds. The two pilots had parachuted into a highly defended area.

Our flight of three started our descent, Sandy Lead first, his wingman, and then our OV-10 following, with a few hundred yards between each aircraft. We flew west of the cloud bank below us, then down to just above treetop level. We headed up a valley, mountains on either side. I remember feeling almost as if I were underwater, in a new world, not the world I'd been viewing for months from a mile high. I looked for antiaircraft fire but saw none. Jingo had been instructed to tell us if we flew anywhere near him. I followed as the A-1Es started to climb back up above the clouds. As we were climbing, Jingo 2-Alpha's voice came through my earphones. He was screaming. "I'm hit, I'm hit." I could hear gunshots in the background. I pictured a caged rabbit, screaming. More gunshots. "I'm hit." Silence. Grim knowledge seeped through me. I felt as if, without electricity, I'd been electrocuted. I felt hollow, placed in nontime. There was no color.

I was getting low on fuel. I informed Sandy that I was bingo. Greg and I returned to base without speaking. We found out that the A-1Es contacted the Bravo and that he too was whispering. Hidden and uninjured. The clouds stayed over the area for two days. Rescue teams stayed above the clouds constantly. After a day, Bravo could no longer be heard on radio, and several days later the search was discontinued. The clouds had not moved away. An informal search lasted several weeks. It was unsuccessful.

Recently I found out, through a Web search, that Jingo 2-Alpha has not been found, but that the backseater, Jingo 2-Bravo, was captured, served as a prisoner of war, and was released in 1973.

I WAS FLYING with a young pilot, Lieutenant Marty Carroll, on his first combat mission. I believe he was the grandson of an Air Force general, or perhaps a son. I don't recall. In any case I had the feeling that he was not happy doing what he was doing but that he was flying out of a sense of duty.

Over Mugia Pass, a highly defended area, we began taking antiaircraft fire.

"Sir," he said, "would you take the aircraft for just a minute?"

"I have the aircraft."

I banked to look for sources of fire, flashes from the ground at the base of an imaginary line of orange tracers, slowly coming from the ground up toward us. I looked into the front seat. Carroll was taking off a glove. He threw up into it, placed it on the floor of the aircraft, and then said, "I have the aircraft, sir."

"Are you sure?"

"Yessir."

After the mission, Carroll seemed upset, quiet.

He was reassigned. I never knew where he went, but I suspect he was unhappy flying combat and was able to get a transfer. If he requested to be relieved of combat duty, then he's the only pilot I ever knew who did so.

DANNY NICHOLS, FRESH from pilot training in the States, became my student. I liked him immediately. I broke him in just as Captain Charles had broken me in. Danny's call sign was Nail 16. He was freckle faced, easy-going, and eager to do well. He was also intelligent and a very good pilot. You could sense that he'd always been an A student, but he had a kind of mischievousness about him that was winning. He was a joy to instruct, one of the best of our new young pilots.

Hoot, besides flying with Prairie Fire, was also an instructor for the Nail FACs, and he flew with Danny a few times.

Hoot recruited Danny for Prairie Fire. And on July 6, 1971, not long after he'd joined, he did not return from a mission. He was due back around 5:30 in the afternoon. By 6:30 those of us in the Nailhole and in headquarters knew that Nail 16 was overdue. Such tardiness was not unheard of. Sometimes a pilot lost hydraulics or electrical power, or even an engine, and diverted to another air base in Thailand. And several hours might pass before we got word.

I remember that I was in a headquarters briefing room, and high on the wall was a small speaker. I sat in a big, soft chair and listened. An announcement with the latest on Nail 16 came every thirty minutes to an hour. I stayed around for a long time to hear good news. It never came.

I learned later that Danny's last radio call came at about 3:30, when he reported that the weather in his area was bad. I've learned since—on the Web—that "a source" reported seeing an OV-10 pilot as a prisoner in Laos a week or so after Danny was last heard from. Some reports say as many as six hundred pilots remain missing in Laos. Other reports say that that number is a consequence of faulty statistical analysis. In any case, many pilots apparently survived crashes and bailouts over Laos, never to be heard from again. A rumor during our combat time was that pilots captured in Laos were beheaded.

I'd begun to think to myself that the reason I flew was to protect my former Yokota roommate, Jim Butts, who was stationed at Da Nang Air Base in South Vietnam. Traditional reasons for warfare were wearing thin. A general feeling among us, though we never said it directly, was that we were losing. I heard rumors of pilots refusing to conduct reconnaissance over highly defended areas unless a strike was scheduled. My rationale for flying combat was that if I did not go out and do my job, then the supplies shipped down the Ho Chi Minh Trail might cause Jim harm or death.

When Danny didn't return from his mission, I decided to write his parents to tell them how much I liked him and what a fine young man he was. It struck me hard: I'd known him well. I kept seeing his face. He was gone, and it was because of the war that he was gone. If we'd not been over there—and I was no longer able to believe we were *defending our country*—if we'd not been over there, Danny would not be missing and very probably dead. I did not have a sense that he had made a sacrifice for something more important than his own life. This was not the way things were supposed to be turning out. Before getting to SEA, I had believed that going to this war was right. After participating—listening, seeing, learning—I didn't.

End of Tour

BEFORE I ARRIVED IN Southeast Asia, several pilots, prior to landing after their last flight, had put on high-speed, low-level air shows. Their tour was over. What could happen? Why not have a little fun? But one of the pilots from another squadron had attempted a low-level loop just before landing and had flown into the ground, killing himself.

The new policy: pilots on their final mission would have an observer along on the flight. The assumption was that the observer could prevent hotdogging. I took a tape recorder and a Super-8 camera on my last mission along with Bob, an O-2 pilot I'd never flown with.

The flight was like most flights except that awaiting me after landing was a bottle of champagne and a dousing with a fire hose from the flight line fire truck.

After several pilots had flown their last flight, a going-home party was held in a back room at the officer's club. Everyone wore his party suit. The party suit was particular

to Southeast Asia, a tailor-made flight suit, black, decorated with an assortment of patches, in addition to our
names over one chest pocket and a small OV-10 over the
other. It was unofficial, paid for by the pilots. A pilot's
motorcycle jacket, I guess. All kinds of patches would be
sewn on party suits—perhaps a map of Southeast Asia on
the back, squadron emblems on the sleeves, a tiger, a
flight school patch, and a personal patch commemorating
a battle or an event or a flight school attended. (Some pilots wore pendants. One I remember was something like
a peace symbol except that the symbol held the word
WAR.) These suits were macho outfits, and most pilots
seemed to enjoy wearing them.

I didn't particularly like the party suits—I was never
fully socialized into the "club"—so when I had mine made
(at a tailor shop off base, where we all had our party suits
made) I asked for no patches except for a small one on my
left shoulder that said BLUE PATCH and a white one on my
right that said WHITE PATCH. The tailor was puzzled. I have
a photo of Hoot Gibson and me in our party suits at my
going-away party. That must have been the night I told
him about almost shooting him down.

IN JULY I OFFICIALLY requested a forty-four-day
rollback; that is, I asked to go home forty-four days short
of my scheduled one-year tour so that I could enter graduate school back in North Carolina in time for the fall semester. I doubted that the request would be granted. Why
should the Air Force do me any favors? But I was wrong.
My request was granted.

At Travis Air Force Base in California I collected a cash payment for my unused leave days.

My days as an United States Air Force pilot were over.

Before flying home to North Carolina, I detoured through New Jersey, where Johnny Hobbs (still a close friend then — and in 2005) was living and flying with the National Guard. We found a Sonny Terry and Brownie McGhee concert in New York City and celebrated. We'd been gone from Yokota for two years. It seemed like a lifetime.

Then I flew home. I was twenty-seven and wanted to do something different.

PART 6

(1984–91)

ANNABELLE

The Purchase and Beyond

IN THE MID-1980s, when I lived in the little town of Apex, North Carolina, a bright yellow Piper Cub flew over my home almost every Sunday afternoon—low and slow. It reminded me of the first airplanes I'd seen as a child.

Since my Air Force days, I'd renewed my pilot's license three times and flown for a few months each time, for a total of less than a hundred hours. I didn't care much for civilian flying; it was a letdown. I'd also taught high school and college and had published two novels. I'd started a third novel, *The Floatplane Notebooks,* which included passages about combat flying. Somehow that writing made me want to fly again or at least be around airplanes.

So one day in 1987 I drove out to the local airfield and happened to see a beautiful little yellow airplane sitting in a hangar—surely the one I'd seen flying around on Sunday afternoons. It sat nose high, unlike modern planes. The third wheel was under the tail, not the nose.

I assumed that all little planes were configured inside

like the Cherokee 140 I'd flown with Mr. Vaughn, or like the T-41 I'd flown when I was still wearing shoes instead of boots with my flight suit in Laredo.

I walked over and looked into the cockpit. There was no yoke, no throttle knob out of the instrument panel. A stick stood on the floor, and the throttle was on the left against the side panel. And not only that: there was room for only one person up front and one person in the back. I'd flown in no civilian aircraft without side-by-side seats. In the T-38, the F-4, and the OV-10 the seating was tandem, just as in this little beauty. I'd be by myself up front or in the back. There were controls in back for flying too. Exactly like a two-seat fighter.

A *strong,* long-dormant urge to fly came thundering back alive after almost twenty years. I *had* to get one of these little airplanes. I *had* to start flying again. Suddenly, as a consequence of form, shape, and memory, I was re-hooked, reinfatuated.

I drove home, ordered flying books, and started reading. I couldn't help it. I read about tail draggers. Since the third wheel is very small and under the tail, the nose sits high. In the old days this high nose kept the propeller away from sand and gravel. It also allowed more room for big propellers, and the high nose set the wings at just the right angle for takeoff.

I saw myself landing a tail dragger on a beach somewhere. I decided that if nothing else I could renew my license again and do some simple civilian flying in a simple civilian aircraft. I drove out to the airfield again and again — and dreamed.

I read more about tail draggers. With the advent of asphalt runways back in the 1940s and 1950s came a new configuration of landing gear. The third wheel, enlarged, was moved to beneath the nose, making these new airplanes much easier to land. I learned that old tail draggers, practically all, were flown with a stick and with the throttle to the left.

A dilemma was that I wanted to fly two passengers rather than just one, yet I wanted to fly alone in the front seat. Perhaps I'd have to settle for a four-seater. The problem seemed insurmountable until I found a book called *The Piper Classics.* In it I read that during the years 1946 and 1947 about thirty-seven hundred PA-12 Super Cruisers had been built, designed with a slightly wider backseat than that of the Piper Cub — wide enough to hold two people. Otherwise it was almost identical to the Cub. I could hardly believe it! The perfect little airplane for me.

I called the Piper dealer in Winston-Salem, North Carolina. I asked him about these Super Cruisers. "Oh, sure," he said. "Would you like to have a list of all PA-12 owners in North Carolina?"

"You bet."

He mailed me the list. There were thirty owners in North Carolina. A quick calculation — fifty states, thirty Super Cruisers per state, fifteen hundred total. Almost 50 percent of them were probably still flying.

I wrote a form letter. It started: "Dear _____, I'd like to buy your airplane."

I sent the letter to each of the thirty owners. I received

five replies. Two replies said something like, "I own a Super Cruiser, it's a wonderful airplane, you're on the right track, but I will never sell mine." The other three owners had Super Cruisers for sale. The first was a "project," meaning it was in separate parts and I'd have to put it together. The second was in Spartanburg, South Carolina, and the third, in Charlotte.

I drove to Spartanburg with my buddy David McGirt, and we looked at the first PA-12 Super Cruiser I ever remembered seeing. I asked the old-timer who owned her to crank her up. I remember watching him climb in. The sound of her engine hypnotized me. I was in love. But the asking price was too much: $16,000. The most I could afford was about $12,000, $14,000 at the very outside.

In the meantime, from a small airport in South Raleigh, I renewed my pilot's license with the prerequisite landings, takeoffs, and air work. I joined AOPA (Aircraft Owners and Pilots Association). I joined a pilots' book club and studied new FAA regulations from books I ordered.

My seven-year-old daughter, Catherine, had never flown before, and when I taxied out to take her up in a rented Cessna for her first ride, she said, "Daddy?"

"Yes?"

"Did you finishing reading that book?"

I GOT TO KNOW the mechanic, Gary Durham, at the Triple W Airport in South Raleigh and found empty hangars there for rent.

I called Jim Council from Charlotte—the third owner wanting to sell. He said he had a sweet-flying PA-12, and he wanted $12,500 for it. It didn't have much in the way of radios and navigational gear, and that's one reason he could offer it for such a good price. He didn't want to sell, but he needed the money.

A few days later I drove to a small airfield near Charlotte and met Jim. He was a pleasant man who seemed sad to sell his plane. We walked over to a row of airplanes under a long, open hangar.

"Here she is," he said. "Want to fly?"

It was a beautiful airplane. White with red trim.

"Sure."

Jim put me in the front seat, got into the back, and talked me through a takeoff. He mentioned the fact that since I'd once flown F-4s, this little airplane should be nothing. At the time I was blissfully unaware of the potential problems of landing a tail dragger, and luckily we had no crosswind on landing. While we were in the air, Jim showed me how sweet she flew, how difficult it was to stall her, and how well she handled. She was unusually stable and steady. I was so eager to own the airplane that I almost made an offer, but I knew I should get my mechanic, Gary, back at South Raleigh, to check her out.

In a few days, Jim flew his airplane to South Raleigh. I stood near the flight building, watching him taxi in, the aircraft nose high and proud. Gary examined the engine and airframe and then took her up for a spin. He landed, taxied in, and motioned for me to walk over to his shop.

"That's one fine little airplane, Clyde," he said. "Very sweet—and in a stall she just keeps flying with the stick pulled back."

"I know," I said. "I'm glad you like her. What do you think about twelve five as an asking price?"

"Very fair. Very fair."

That morning I'd written three checks and stuffed them into my shirt pocket. The check on top was for $11,000; the next, for $11,500; and the third, for the asking price, $12,500. I'd bargain with Jim, strike a deal, pull the $11,000 or maybe the $11,500 from my pocket, and save myself some money. Yessir.

I walked from Gary's hangar, across the lawn, over to the flight building. Jim was inside, sitting near a stove with a couple of other fellows.

"Jim," I said, "could we walk out to the plane?"

"Sure."

We walked out the door and started across the lawn toward the little plane I would name *Annabelle*. It was a cold, clear January day.

I said, "Jim, I want to make you an offer for your airplane."

"Sure."

"I want to offer you eleven thousand dollars."

"Well . . . Clyde, I really need the money. I hate to sell this airplane, and I need twelve thousand five hundred."

"Okay," I said, reaching for the bottom check.

We shook hands.

"Let's go back inside," he said, "and I'll sign it over to you."

We sat at a small table inside, away from the others. Jim filled out the title, and where it asked for price, he wrote, "$1 poc." "That means one dollar plus other costs," he said. "That way nobody knows what you paid, in case you want to sell her."

"I don't think that's going to happen."

He signed the title and pushed it over to me to sign. As he turned to look out the window, I saw tears in his eyes. I signed the title, folded it, put it in my pocket. I believe his sadness was as low as my joy was high.

"I'll take good care of her," I said.

In a rented Cessna I flew Jim back to his home airfield. I couldn't fly my airplane because I had no insurance on it. A few days earlier I'd called the insurance folks, expecting no problems. I was certainly qualified, I thought. When I separated from the Air Force, I had a private license, a commercial rating, an instrument rating, a multi-engine rating, and about fourteen hundred hours of flying time.

After I explained my qualifications, my new insurance agent asked for the make and model of the aircraft I wanted to insure.

"A Piper Super Cruiser," I said. "A PA-Twelve."

"You'll need ten hours of instruction in that aircraft before we can insure you."

"What? . . . Why?"

"You'll see," he said.

The "you'll see" was about the tail wheel. As mentioned, the third wheel of most modern airplanes is under the nose, and the placement of the two main landing gear (more toward the rear than on a tail dragger) means the modern aircraft is heavier in front of the main gear than behind. The weight not resting on the main landing gear rests on that nose gear. This helps the aircraft to continue moving forward in a straight line after landing.

But with a tail dragger the ballast is behind the main gear. And that can cause control problems after landing.

Yet in the air, both types fly the same.

Think about throwing an arrow with the feathers out front and the arrowhead in the rear. After it's thrown, the arrow will reverse ends. A tail dragger, on the ground, will tend to do the same, especially if a crosswind blows the tail to the left or right just after the plane lands. In that case, as the tail moves to the left or right, the airplane is of course pivoting on the main landing gear and heading in the direction it's pointing. Without rapid correction, the tail will tend to keep moving to the left or right and on around in front of the nose. It's called a ground loop. What aids the tail in heading around to the front of the nose is (1) that initial weather-vaning and (2) the weight being behind the main gear.

Additionally, the nose is so high in front of the pilot on most tail draggers that a clear view straight ahead for taxiing is not possible. You must zigzag to see where you're going. (In the air, a tail dragger levels out just like a nose-wheel aircraft, and you can see over the nose just fine.)

I asked my mechanic, Gary, if he knew of an instructor who could check me out in a tail dragger.

"You're lucky," he said. "They're hard to come by, but we've got one right here at South Raleigh: Waldo Ricks."

Waldo was what the doctor ordered. He was older, with many hours in many kinds of airplanes, and lots of time in tail draggers. He was salty and a bit acerbic, and he loved to sit and talk flying. He agreed to instruct me for my required ten hours.

"Do you think I need ten hours?" I asked.

"I do."

After our first flight, Waldo was also in love with *Annabelle*. "What a sweet-flying machine," he said.

My ten hours were spent learning to handle *Annabelle* just after touchdown in a crosswind. Waldo taught me how to aggressively stomp on the rudder to stay straight down the runway rather than weather-vaning into the wind, and how to pin the tail wheel aggressively to the ground.

Often, when I flew *Annabelle* into a little airfield, an old-timer sitting in the flight building would ask, "Ground-looped her yet?"

"No, sir."

Silence. Then another would say, "Well, it ain't a matter of 'if.' It's a matter of 'when.'"

"Yessir." But I didn't believe it. Ground loop? Not me, brother.

Waldo and I finished our ten hours. We had a good time flying—he would laugh as I tried to wrestle *Annabelle* in a crosswind landing—and after my ten hours were up, Waldo piloted *Annabelle* on his own a few times, just for the thrill. He didn't get the opportunity to fly many tail draggers. And after he'd finished with my instruction, I enjoyed sitting in the flight shack, listening to him tell stories. He told me a story about insurance one day. I wrote it in my journal.

"I told my ex-wife when we got divorced and she got the

dog that I'd get rid of that dog if I were her. Saint Bernard. If you don't breed them right, they're vicious. They get good press as gentle dogs, but they come from breeds that were used to fight the gladiators.

"So I'm working in the pansies, right before the divorce, and the dog is tied with a logging chain to a porch railing set in bricks and cement, and this German shepherd walks by and I think, 'Thank God, the Saint Bernard is chained,' and the German shepherd gets about three feet in the yard, and the Saint Bernard pulls up the railing and in about one and a half minutes there's nothing left of the German shepherd but fur, blood, and bones.

"Three years later I meet my former brother-in-law at the airport. We have breakfast. He says something about insurance. Then he says the next victim was a lady walking by and she was about to undergo her second round of corrective surgery."

We sit for a minute. "What's that got to do with insurance?" I ask.

"Oh. USAA has a thirty-dollar rider to homeowners that is good for a million dollars on any injury liability."

"And?"

"I don't know. That's just a story about insurance. I hope she had it."

ANNABELLE WAS WHITE with red trim, as I've mentioned, and she had a red and black interior. She was a work of art. Her skin was smooth, painted fabric stretched tightly over wood. A special fuel-and-leather-fabric smell lingered in her interior. Her wings were long, and a wingtip was as high as your head. You could take the wingtip in hand and rock her. You could walk to the rear and pick the rear end off the ground and turn her in a circle.

I enjoyed washing and cleaning her inside and out, polishing the red and white metal "fenders" over her main gear.

I often just walked around her, looking, admiring. Then I'd stand off at a distance and stare.

I WAS RENTING a fully enclosed metal hangar at Triple W Airport in South Raleigh when a pilot friend asked me to hop in *Annabelle* and follow him and his Cessna to a little hideaway airfield about thirty minutes away: there was a hangar for rent there. I followed him into Decker Field, landing on a green turf runway in the woods. I met the owner of the field, Phil Decker, a farmer, carpenter, airplane mechanic, and antique aircraft rebuilder. At the field was a large metal hangar, where Phil worked on airplanes. Across the runway stood a small wooden hangar, where an empty space rented for forty dollars a month. I took it.

The hangar was low slung, wide enough for three airplanes, the two outside airplanes facing in one direction and the middle one (mine) facing in the opposite direction. My taxi-out path, behind the hangar, was slightly downhill. So upon returning from a flight, I'd taxi around back by a vegetable garden to my entrance and do a tight turnaround with rudder, brake, and revved-up engine so that the tail of *Annabelle* faced the opening. At the rear wall of my hangar space was a hand winch—just like the one on a boat trailer. I'd attach the winch's long metal wire to a towing handle on the tail of the aircraft and slowly crank her into the hangar.

All this was wonderfully anti–Air Force, antimodern, antitechnological. Not only that, but Waldo had taught me to start the engine by hand in case of battery-operated starter problems. You've seen old black-and-white films in which one person sits in an airplane while another person, standing in front of the airplane, puts both hands on the propeller and then heaves mightily and immediately backs away. The secret is to use both hands and then get out of the way. On many cold mornings, after several failed attempts to battery-start, I'd set my hand brake, leave the ignition switch on, prime the engine with a little bit of throttle, get out, drift back in time to those old films, place my hands up on the propeller, heave down, crank her up, jump back, jump in, and fly away.

A typical takeoff at Decker Field went like this: I'd crank my engine and taxi to the north end of the runway. Takeoff was always in the same direction—south—because the relatively short turf runway was *downhill* to the south. No advantage could be gained by taking off uphill—regardless of wind direction. As I taxied along the edge of the field toward the north end of the runway, I'd come to a dogleg to the right. I'd taxi around the corner there, continue ten or fifteen yards to the end of the runway at the edge of the woods, turn 180 degrees, stop, and complete my before-takeoff checklist, which included applying brakes, opening the throttle to see if I was getting full rpm, and checking all instruments.

Then I would release the brakes with the power wide open and start a slow roll. Immediately I'd round the corner of the dogleg to the left—just getting rolling good—and see the entire runway, sloping downhill, in front of me. I could reduce power and apply brakes if something was in the way. But if the runway was clear and no one was coming in to land (landing was always *uphill* at Decker Field—to the north), I would continue my takeoff roll.

Before liftoff I would cross the gravel driveway to Phil's house—a little bump—and then after a few seconds I'd be airborne. If I was making a short-field takeoff, then the whole time I was rolling along I'd hold the stick as far back between my legs as it would go so that as soon as flying speed was reached, the airplane lifted into the air. Then I'd immediately move the stick forward to a position for a comfortable climb-out.

This slow, low-flying tail dragger made little sense to most civilian pilots I knew. Their airplanes with tricycle landing gear were faster and always much easier to maneuver on the ground. They liked to go places. They liked technology. But I liked to linger above green fields, to find turf landing strips, to fly a traffic pattern over and over and over, practicing touch-and-go landings. I liked the simplicity of the PA-12. I liked being forced to navigate by time and distance, with a map in my lap, rather than by instruments that (with modern satellite technology) give location and route directions. I was proud to taxi into an airport, get out, walk into the lounge, and have somebody ask, "What kind of airplane is that? Where'd you get it? Is it fun?"

Just after buying *Annabelle* in 1989, I moved books, a couch, and a desk into a small, windowless office in a building on Ninth Street in Durham, North Carolina, my hometown. The office was a quiet place to write fiction, my full-time job back then—which explains in part why I had time to fly. After moving into the office, I needed a sign on the door. I came upon the idea of a kind of informal air taxi service. I could make it a nonprofit. If someone wanted to go somewhere, I'd fly them for cost. I tried out several names: Happy's Air Taxi, Billy's Air Taxi, Orville's Air Taxi. Nothing quite worked. Finally, I settled on Dusty's Air Taxi. I liked the irony: a "Dusty" would be earthy, uneasy in the sky.

At that time, 1989, I'd just finished writing *The Floatplane Notebooks*. In that book a character keeps notebooks about a floatplane he's building.

The Floatplane Notebooks

ONE SUMMER DAY BACK in 1984, five years before I bought *Annabelle,* I was standing in the upper parking lot at Lake Wheeler, a popular lake near my house. Down the hill toward the lake, in a lower parking lot, I saw a parked pickup truck with a boat trailer attached. On the trailer rested something that looked like a small boat with long, folded back wings. Up front, attached to the frame, were two propellers. I could see somebody moving around in the cab of the pickup. I walked down to take a closer look. Yes, it was, by golly, some kind of aircraft.

In the small open cockpit was a flight stick up from the floor, rudder pedals, throttles to the left, and an airspeed indicator on the tiny instrument panel. And there, in glory, sat the pilot's seat: a bolted-to-the-floor, yellow and green *aluminum lawn chair.*

I walked to the open driver's door of the pickup truck. Inside was a small man with thin, wispy red hair. He wore fishing waders and was pulling a blue football helmet onto his head. That's right: he was wearing fishing waders and was pulling a blue football helmet onto his head. I introduced myself, reached into the cab, and shook his hand.

"Tom Purcell," he said. "Pleased to meet you."

"Are you going to try to fly that thing?"

"I sure am." He got out of the truck and looked up at me. He was intense and had a twinkle in his eye. He looked obsessed somehow, slightly worried, busy, preoccupied.

"Can I help you out in any way?" I asked.

"As a matter of fact, you can. Once I get it in the water and get in it, you can hold me at the dock there until I get her cranked and running."

"Do you . . . just . . . fold those wings out?"

"Yep. They snap right into place."

Then he gave me a walk-around tour of his creation, and as we walked I got happier and happier. This was magic.

Mr. Purcell backed his boat-trailered aircraft down into the water. I was standing on a dock, holding on to a rope attached to a lanyard hoop on the nose of the aircraft as it floated out into the water. Mr. Purcell parked his truck, came back, walked into the water, and carefully unfolded and locked the flimsy-looking aluminum and canvas wings into place. From the dock, he climbed down onto the aircraft nose, then into his aluminum lawn chair, and after I turned the aircraft around to face out toward the lake, he asked me to hold it by its tail.

"Don't turn her loose until I give you the signal," he said.

Down on my knees on the dock, I held on to the tail section while he produced from somewhere a short lawn mower starting cord with a handle at one end and a knot in the other. Even 1984 was a late date to be using such a cord.

I wondered if he had a paddle, but I didn't ask.

He wrapped the starter rope on the circular cranker of the left chain saw engine and pulled. Nothing. He pulled again. Nothing. I was holding on. Again. And again. He tried the right engine. *Wee-aaang. Wang-wang-wang-wang.* He looked at me and smiled.

I thought to myself, He's happy *about getting one engine started.*

He tried again and started the other engine. Both propellers were spinning. I felt only a slight tug away from the dock. He looked at me again. He was obviously pleased.

He fastened his seat belt and surveyed the cockpit, almost as if to say good-bye to it. He raised both hands and pointed his index fingers seaward. I turned the little flying boat loose and stood back. Throttles forward, it started moving away, out onto the lake, slowly picking up speed. *Weeeennnnggg.* Out across the water it continued. Would it suddenly lift and fly? Would it suddenly lift and not fly?

Weeeeennngg. Soon it was leaving a wake, bouncing, throwing up splats of water from each side. Far across the lake, nearing land, it slowed, and then I heard the engines wind down. It turned and began to pick up speed . . . headed not directly back at me, but at an angle to my right. Full steam ahead, again. The sudden high whine of the engines reached me across the water. Several times, it crossed a boat wake and seemed to bounce into the air, but only for a split second.

Back and forth, back and forth, but it never flew. Returning to the dock with his hand lifted in greeting, Mr. Purcell seemed no less pleased with himself and his creation.

AT HOME THAT NIGHT, I made notes. I was a treasure-hunting fiction writer who'd just found a sunken, gold-laden ship — or rather, a nonflying, lawn-chair-laden floatplane.

After several attempts at short stories about a homemade floatplane, I realized that the strange homebuilt craft could fit into my novel-in-progress, then called *Natural Suspension.*

Seeing that homebuilt floatplane was one of the best things that ever happened to me. It provided vivid and significant fodder for a novel in need of vivid and significant fodder. The floatplane would belong to the likable yet clumsy head of the Copeland family household, Albert. So I wrote a floatplane into my novel, but I soon deserted that novel to write another, *Walking Across Egypt.*

When I returned to the floatplane book, I decided to track down Mr. Purcell, although several years had passed since my floatplane sighting and I'd forgotten his name.

I called the main gate at Lake Wheeler. No, the gate-keeper didn't remember anybody flying a homebuilt aircraft off the lake, but somebody in the Aeronautical Department at North Carolina State University would probably know. I called a chaplain friend at State and asked for the phone number of the Aeronautical Department. He looked. No such department, he said, but there was a Mechanical and Aeronautical Engineering Department. He gave me the number, and I spoke to the department chair. He told me he didn't know anything about a homebuilt aircraft at Lake Wheeler, but there was a member of his department who might. He gave me a name and number, and I called. No, sorry—but there was another member of the department who might be able to help me. Several days had passed by this time.

"No, I don't know of a homebuilt airplane flying off Lake Wheeler, but there's a man at the Department of Transportation here in Raleigh who I'll bet could help you: Marshall Sanderson. Here's his phone number."

I called Mr. Sanderson, described what I'd seen several years earlier, and asked if he might know the gentleman trying to fly the homebuilt floatplane.

Silence. "Did he have red hair?"

"Yessir, he did. Kind of thin red hair."

"That would be Tom Purcell. I'll give you his phone number."

When Mr. Purcell answered the phone, I explained who I was and asked if he remembered the day in question.

"I sure do," he said. "That particular aircraft never got off the water, and I finally dismantled it and with some of the parts built a new floatplane—and that one never flew either. But with parts of the second, I built a third, and she's flying just fine. Would you like to see it?"

"Well, of course." I told him I was working on a novel,

and in the novel a character owned an airplane similar to the one I'd seen at Lake Wheeler. Could I ask him a few questions?

He was happy to talk and invited me to his office. Before he hung up, he said, "I've got some notebooks you can examine. They tell the whole story."

Notebooks?

My novel, still without a title, needed structure, a thread, to somehow hold all its scenes and stories together. I immediately imagined my character Albert Copeland keeping a flying notebook, and because the novel was in many ways about a family, I saw that his keeping such a notebook, entering nontechnical "family" notes in it, could be exactly the thread my novel needed. So I made up notebook entries and put them here and there in the novel, then called my editor and told her about the added notebooks. Since we were looking for a title for the book, I suggested *The Floatplane Notebooks*. She liked the title, and it stuck.

To visit Mr. Purcell before I finished the book offered me a chance for new material, but I didn't want to risk another year of working on a novel I'd been wrestling with off and on for almost a decade. So I finished the book, *then* visited Mr. Purcell.

I found him in a small office with adjoining workrooms near the Raleigh-Durham Airport. He loved to talk flying, and I loved to listen. He once had dinner with Orville Wright. He'd invented a kind of glider for the Army during World War II; it was launched from larger aircraft high in the air so that it could glide along and finally land behind enemy lines. (A glider—*behind* enemy lines?!) He had designed a device to reduce vibration in nuclear power plants. He showed me pictures and diagrams of his inventions and projects. Finally he showed me his floatplane notebooks.

"Take a look through them if you like," he said.

I thumbed through the notebooks and found his entry for his first successful flight in his third-generation homebuilt. It went something like this: "The aircraft lifted off and flew about one hundred yards. I taxied back and, just before reaching the dock, ran out of fuel." I flipped through a few pages and found hand-drawn charts and diagrams and short statements like "This didn't work, so I tried this."

It was as if he'd used my character's notebooks as a guide. They were both—all three of us, actually—delighted to put words on paper about this business of getting into the air in a flying machine.

The *Annabelle* Notebooks

AT SOME POINT DURING the reign of Dusty's Air Taxi, I began keeping a notebook of my own, about flying my own airplane, *Annabelle*. It was written in the spirit of Tom Purcell's and Albert Copeland's notebooks—dry, terse, third-person accounts.

17 Nov 89. First flight of the air taxi service after its establishment on 7 Nov 1989. Purpose of flight was to transport the pilot to Hot Springs, Va., for a reading of his fiction at a conference of the Virginia Library Association. Passenger along for the ride was Michael McFee. Takeoff was scheduled for 8:30 a.m. or 0830 hours. The aircraft would not start with the battery-operated starter. A hand start was attempted and was successful at 0940. Takeoff was at 0946 hours. Passenger experienced minor discomforts due to cold air and rough air. Visibility was good. Destination airfield (Ingalls Field, Hot Springs, Va.) was along the northeastern end of a mountaintop, and at the end of the

runway was a cliff. An exciting place to land. At 1500, hand-start attempts for flight back to N.C. proved unsuccessful because of cold weather. Pilot and passenger rented automobile. 21 Nov. was planned return.

20 Nov. West Virginia aircraft mechanic reported on phone that aircraft was battery-started without incident, with master switch in down/on position rather than up/on position. Return trip by auto to retrieve aircraft postponed until 25 Nov 89 because of inclement weather. Snow.

22 Nov 89. Services of aerial photographer obtained for future uses when called upon. David McGirt of Buies Creek, N.C.

27 Nov 89. Pilot and passenger Tim McLaurin drove rental car 5½ hours to Ingalls Field, Va., to recover aircraft. En route Mr. Edgerton and Mr. McLaurin were lost twice and received one speeding ticket. Arrived at 1200 hours. First attempt to start *Annabelle,* after snow and ice removal, was unsuccessful, though it was determined that battery and starter were connected via master switch in down/on position. Aircraft was pushed into a large hangar by Edgerton, McLaurin, and two locals. Engine cowling was opened. Electrical power was available in hangar. Various extension cords enabled the positioning of a hair dryer blowing on left magneto and one on right. Space heater was placed on an oilcan sitting below engine so as to be near engine. A plastic extension hose directed air from heater into bottom cowling opening. A 2-amp battery recharger was connected to battery. Openings in cowling that would allow cold air entry/heat escape were stuffed with NFL Dolphins jacket, bath towels, a

sleeping bag, and a sweater. Long-handle underwear were stuffed around air intake; two sleeping bags covered cowling on outside. Object was to heat engine. All apparati were brought from N.C. or purchased en route (hose and duct tape). After one hour of heating, 1245–1345, all apparati were removed/disconnected, switches turned on. Aircraft started instantly when starter button was touched. At 1210 pilot took off without incident, flew to Decker Field with touch-and-go landing at Person County Airport just south of Roxboro, N.C. Touchdown at Decker Field: 1600. Income from first Dusty's Air Taxi venture: $60, Virginia Library Association. Expenses: Aircraft fuel and oil, $60; mechanic, $125; auto fuel, $25; Virginia Highway Patrol, $68; food, $25; duct tape and hose, $5.31; Hertz, $367.

For some reason (embarrassment?) I wrote no comments in my notebook about the return flight above. Tim was in the backseat. After takeoff I was navigating out of the mountains. Something was wrong. I was lost—in the rugged mountains. I did not realize that my compass was malfunctioning. Interference from a new radio was throwing the compass off by about thirty-five degrees. I kept finding myself unable to match my map (specific river bends, railroad crossings, and so forth) with what was below me on the ground. I didn't consider that the compass was wrong. I was mumbling about the problem when Tim, behind me, asked, "What's wrong?"

I told him.

He said, "I've got a compass."

I turned and looked over my shoulder. He was pulling a necklace from inside his shirt, and dangling from it was a small compass.

"What direction do you need to fly?" he asked.

"Almost south," I said. "About one hundred fifty degrees." I waited.

"Well, you need to go that way."

I looked back.

He was pointing.

Soon we saw a water tower below. I buzzed it. SOUTH BOSTON (a town in southern Virginia) was written on the side. I knew where we were, and found our way home.

2 Dec 89. Chief pilot and seven-year-old daughter, Catherine, drove to Decker Field with chest of drawers in pickup truck to be installed in hangar. Items in chest of drawers included cleansers, cleaning rags and towels, tools, life preservers—orange—for extended over-water flight, lightbulbs for engine heating, extension cords, small rechargeable vacuum cleaner, windshield cover from previous owner, and other useful items. Pilot and daughter started aircraft and took off at approximately 1600 hours for 30-minute training flight in local area. The following were executed: several lazy 8s, several steep-banked turns, a power-on stall, a power-off stall, a spiraling turn. The passenger expressed enjoyment of all maneuvers. The landing was, of necessity, with a tailwind. The pilot placed 200-watt bulb in engine, with cowling openings stopped up with rags, towels, sponges—for experiment on following morning.

3 Dec 89. Following experiment was successful: starting engine. After a cold night. With lightbulb for overnight heat.

6 Dec 89. Gary Hawkings, filmmaker, questioned the chief pilot at Decker Field. Pilot sat on a stool in front of *Annabelle*. Questions regarded Tim McLaurin, Dusty's program development chair and part-time navigator. Gary was making a film called *The Rough South of Tim McLaurin*. After the interview, the pilot took the filmmaker for a short, filmed ride around the field.

7 Dec 89. Mission to Fayetteville put on hold due to inclement weather: snow.

9 Dec 89. Mission to Fayetteville postponed again. Weather.

14 Dec 89. Plans made for Dusty's first annual meeting and planning session, for Sunday, Dec. 17, at 1730. Place to be determined.

17 Dec. 1830 hours. First annual meeting and planning session. Another Thyme Restaurant in Durham, N.C. First two choices, In the Raw on the Eno and Weeping Radish, were closed. Attending: C. Edgerton, pilot; D. McGirt, aerial photographer. Displayed: Dusty's Air Taxi's first aerial photographs, which were of North Carolina's Outer Banks. Discussed: photography and air-to-air combat. Meeting adjourned 1930 hours.

11 Jan 1990. Chief pilot took daughter for aircraft ride to Chapel Hill, purchased Dr Pepper and small bag of potato chips for her. One landing in Chapel Hill. On return flight, pilot accomplished lazy 8s, steep-banked turns, power-off stalls, and slow flight.

On postflight, pilot failed to tie down aircraft. Returned to field and did so. High winds forecast for 12 Jan. One bulb and battery charger left in place, no cowling stuffing.

22 Aug 90. A mouse chewed up into little pieces a candy bar wrapper left in the aircraft.

Office to Remain Open

MY FRIEND WITH THE compass around his neck, Tim McLaurin, glimpsed a copperhead crossing the road one day and realized he didn't have his ever-ready pillowcase (snake carrier) with him in his pickup truck. So when he caught the snake, he held it in his right hand by the neck so that it couldn't bite him, and drove toward home with his left. As he turned into his driveway, the snake wriggled loose enough to bite Tim on the middle joint of his right index finger.

We talked on the phone. He was in the hospital, but he downplayed the whole incident.

When I visited him, Tim, still in bed, held up his hand and arm for me to inspect. The arm was twice its normal size, his tattoo spread wide, and at first I thought the finger was wrapped in black leather. It wasn't—that was skin.

He survived, of course, but he wasn't as lucky as he'd been when he was simultaneously bitten by two rattlesnakes a few years back. He'd been feeding them. They "knew" him, he claimed, and thus the bites had been dry, without venom.

Tim died of cancer in 2002, and I lost a true and valued friend. He and I flew together in *Annabelle* several times after that day back in 1989 when he pulled the compass up from around his neck. One day not long after that trip, he said, "How about you fly me down to Wilmington to buy four rattlesnakes?"

An image came into my head: the two of us in *Annabelle*'s tiny cockpit, he in the rear, and I up front—and somewhere in there with us, a wooden cage or cooler holding four rattlesnakes. The next image came to me: the six of us in an upside-down crashed airplane that was about to catch on fire—Tim and I hanging upside down by our seat belts with the snakes loose below our heads on the ceiling.

I did not want to say no to Tim's request. But I didn't want to say yes either. So I changed the subject. I'd like to think that if pressured, I would have said yes.

The image of two guys hanging upside down by their seat belts in an airplane about to catch fire with snakes waiting for them on the ceiling seemed ripe for fiction. So I wrote a short story about that and then later rewrote it as a scene for the novel *In Memory of Junior*.

JIM HENDERSON, ANOTHER FRIEND, and I were about to go for a ride. It was Monday, January 21, 1991, Martin Luther King Jr. Day. Jim wanted to take aerial photographs of the Friends School that his son and my daughter attended, and I was happy to offer the aerial platform. As usual, I called the weather station at Raleigh-Durham Airport. The reported wind was fifteen knots out of the north. My rule was not to fly if the ground wind was fifteen knots or more. As explained, landing a tail dragger in high wind is tricky and dangerous.

Good sense, safe sense, dictated that I not fly that day. The wind was too strong. But I was confident and ready to fly. I'd yet to have a cheap lesson about "confidence." Even though Raleigh-Durham was the official weather station for the area, perhaps I could cheat. I called another airport, Person County Airport, five miles north of Decker Field, and asked about the winds there. Twelve knots out of the north. Good, I would fly.

I finished my preflight check, we climbed in, I cranked, and we taxied out of the hangar to the end of the runway, which was around that short dogleg.

On takeoff roll, the aircraft felt slow and heavy. Because of the high tailwind, the roll was very long. We lifted off. *Annabelle* was not climbing well. Far across a field ahead loomed a line of tall trees. I'd become uneasy during the long roll, and now I visualized not clearing the trees. I immediately aborted the takeoff, dropping *Annabelle* back down onto the runway. But we were almost out of runway and moving along at a good clip. No problem, I thought, because beyond the runway was an open field. I'd walked over it soon after renting my hangar. What I didn't know was that since then, a ditch had been dug perpendicular to our ground path. We rolled into the field and *Annabelle*'s main landing gear dropped into the ditch.

The rear of the airplane lifted into the air and continued over the nose, as if in slow motion. *Ka-wham*. We landed upside down. I'd ground-looped—tail over head.

We hung upside down from our seat belts.

I had bumped my head somehow. I was stunned. I asked Jim if he was okay. He said he'd cut his head, but not badly. I turned and looked. He was staring at his hand. A bit of blood was on his fingertips. We unbuckled our seat belts, fell into the top of the cockpit, then scrambled out.

I stood and looked at my love, *Annabelle*. Totaled.

THAT NIGHT I CALLED several friends to tell them about the crash—Jim Butts, Johnny Hobbs, David McGirt. Was I okay? they asked. How was the airplane? What happened? Still shaken, I told each of them the story.

I called Tim. "Tim, I crashed my airplane today."

"Damn," he said. "I wish I'd been with you."

HERE'S THE FINAL Dusty's Air Taxi notebook entry:

21 Jan 91. Aircraft disabled on aborted takeoff, later declared a total loss, as a consequence of estimate of repair costs. Insufficient power was available to complete takeoff climb under conditions at the time. Decision was made at about 10–20 feet in the air to abort takeoff and climb-out. Aircraft was landed. Aircraft rolled beyond end of runway (Decker Field) into a field. When main landing gear entered a shallow ditch, the gear remained stationary and the aircraft

continued onto nose and then onto top, leaving pilot and passenger, photographer Jim Henderson, with bumps on heads and suspended in seat belts upside down.

Egress was accomplished, hastily.

FAA inspection determined the mishap to be an incident rather than an accident.

Flight operations temporarily suspended. Office to remain open.

PART 7

(2003–05)

LOOKING BACK

Hippie Dance

WHEN I STARTED PILOT training in 1966, the national anti-war movement was little more that a national whisper. By the time I got my wings in 1967, a more public antiwar movement was getting under way. That year had been a crowded, heady year for me. There'd been little time for anything outside studying flying, thinking flying, breathing flying. I'd been unable to keep up with news about the antiwar movement, but by 1968–69 that movement and the 1960s revolution were beginning to interest me and some of my buddies stationed in Japan, flying F-4s. Every Wednesday night at the officer's club we danced to the music of Janis Joplin and her band, Big Brother and the Holding Company, as performed by another band from the States. In our quarters, my roommate, Jim, would lie on the floor between his big stereo speakers, listening to the Doors' "Light My Fire." On our refrigerator was that peace symbol, and on our walls, the antiwar poster. So by

1969 there was a kind of unspoken peace between anti-war demonstrators and certain pilots, of whom I was one.

Then a year later in Clovis, New Mexico, there were enough of us in this contingent to decide on, plan, and execute a hippie dance. One night we cleared two rooms in the BOQ, set up a stereo system, gathered tapes and records, and had us a dance. Guys brought wives or girl-friends. We were all hippies, and we were not being disrespectful (of hippies), or at least some of us weren't, I know. I filmed it with my Super-8 camera. The movie shows pilots dressed as hippies, dancing. Hippie spirit was contagious. And fun.

The next morning, as I climbed into my old T-33, smelled aircraft fuel and old metal, pulled on my helmet, attached my G suit, started engines, pulled my oxygen mask to my face, and checked in on the radio, "Silver Two," hippie spirit vanished.

Courage

THE VIETNAM WAR FOLLOWS me around like a small, dark, deadly cloud, just over my shoulder. My part in the war floats somewhere in that cloud, accompanied by remnants of fear, pride, shame, exhilaration, and sadness. Without my dream of being a pilot, I might have missed the war.

When I look back, I am surprised at my nonchalance about being ready to drop a nuclear weapon on Russian soil if commanded to do so. Did I ever contemplate the fact that hundreds of young men like me were, without one question, preparing to follow probably self-annihilating commands from their superiors, and might be responsible for bringing about a horrible end to world civilization — civilization, that state in which human beings marry, have children, live safely in homes where they perhaps achieve some kind of meaning and happiness, make plans to go fishing, build tree houses, play ball, and go outside and enjoy the green mist of buds in spring trees while eating a sandwich?

No. I did not contemplate any such thing.

How can a young man, raised in the Baptist Church, learning the *teachings of Jesus,* soaking in the pleasures and joys of being alive on Earth, the joys of eating, loving, sharing, laughing—how can he race toward an aircraft carrying a nuclear bomb to be dropped on other human beings, many of whom he would clearly like, even love, if given the chance? Is such willingness to kill in our genes, irrevocable? What gets us whipped into such a frenzy, and how much can we ever do about it?

THE WRITING OF THIS book has been the third chapter in my flying life. The first was military flying; the second was *Annabelle;* and now I am trying to separate the wheat from the chaff, to understand why I chose to go to war, to examine the pride, the shame, and the exhilaration and to see how they have worked for, against, and around one another.

In 1994, before writing this book allowed me to better understand my part in war and my journey to war, I visited the Vietnam Veterans Memorial in Washington, D.C. The memorial is not a statue of a great steed, a great soldier, a great eagle, a great sword; there is no giant symbol to give rise to passion and nationalism. The wall speaks differently. It is only what it is: a wall—with the names of those once alive among us who died in the war in Vietnam. It is a record, a narrative of names.

I stood before it the first time, almost numb. When I

found the name I was looking for—that of the young man I'd trained who became my friend and who never returned from his mission that day back in 1971—a sudden release and collapse of something deep inside me brought a rush of tears and a long moan. I felt possessed by an inside self suddenly grown big, a kind of gangly self, breaking out into the open, taking over, unable to hold back anguish any longer.

I turned away, my face in my hands, and found myself almost violently embraced by a man I'd never seen. He said, "It's all right, brother. I understand."

He held me for a long ten or fifteen seconds and then turned me loose. He was crying too.

As I quickly came back to myself, I was embarrassed to have been held by someone I didn't know. He stepped away, then walked over and embraced someone else. He brought me comfort in that moment, and I wonder if he understood what I felt. He may have been full of pride that he'd fought in Vietnam. I don't know. I wasn't. And I'm not now.

Pride in my combat flying has dimmed as I have looked back on my nation's role in Southeast Asia, yet the memories of my youthful excitement about learning to fly military aircraft are somehow still bright. That early seduction into war needs to be told.

Aeons ago when we had no tools of war beyond sticks and stones, the consequence of armed conflict was not usually massive death. The advent of manned flight, especially, has changed all that. And we don't seem to mind selling our war technology and instruction to other nations. In my pilot training class was an Iranian student pilot.

A search of history—of ourselves—to find reason for hope in these matters is not comforting. As George Santayana said, "Only the dead have seen the end of war."

The life of an enemy civilian—mother, son, daughter, father—gets lost in the strategy of war and the viewing of war, whether through scopes, bomb sights, or television cameras. Real life, the feel of it, the skin, the blood, the hope to live, is lost in translation.

Will leaders holding the reins to war ever learn to listen well to the enemies' civilians? Put themselves in their places? Know how religion, culture, traditions, have shaped these civilians, their aspirations?

If an American Indian had interviewed me when I was eighteen, would I have been able to explain the fact that so much of my boyhood—playtime, reading time, movie-viewing time—was spent killing pretend Indians or reading about their being killed or seeing them killed because they were all *bad,* and not worth much? And my enjoyment in killing pretend Indians was not because they were a threat—we'd already killed God knows how many of them over a couple of hundred years. Part of my enjoyment came from the fact that I had a young, impressionable human heart in my time (the 1950s and 1960s) and place (an America where non-Caucasians were often considered inferior and were advertised as such).

The need of soldiers to depersonalize the enemy (*gook, gomer*) is as old as war. And why is that? Because humans sometimes find it hard to live with what they do—killing people, other soldiers, even—as they do it.

War machines have killed millions of young men, women,

old people, and babies during the last century. Every major industrialized nation has a machine. Certain moving parts of the machine, young men and women, are no braver, no better, no worse, generally, than the youngsters in the camp of the enemy. Leaders with power mistrust one another, manufacture slogans, taunt and mislead, and instigate battles they will not have to fight in—alongside youngsters who die dreaming of home and heroism.

Army, Air Force, Navy, and Marine recruitment commercials touch on the need for little boys, and now girls, to be heroes. They do not advertise the killing of other human beings.

FOR MY PART in the failed attempt to rescue Jingo 2-Alpha and 2-Bravo, I won a Distinguished Flying Cross. In that way I became a hero. After the mission that day, I was asked by our awards officer if I wanted to be written up for a Silver Star (next after the Medal of Honor). I doubted that I deserved a Silver Star, and I liked the way a Distinguished Flying Cross (next in line) looked. It was shaped like an airplane propeller. I said, "No, I'll take a DFC. I think they're neat."

"Well," he said, "write down what happened."

In 2003, my second child, a son, was born. My wife, Kristina, and I took care of him during his first month while I took a break from teaching and writing, and at one point we were also in charge, for a day, of our two-year-old nephew. For a while I was in charge of both the toddler and the infant. This experience, the details and demands, made me think of all the women worldwide who, alone, care for children, and it made me consider how we tend to define courage.

A man with an airplane flies into the air, into physical danger. Let's say his mission is a combat mission. The chances are he will return, and when he does, he will have enjoyed the flight—probably in direct proportion to the danger he faced and evaded during the flight. And even if he didn't "enjoy" it, he will enjoy discussing it, re-living it, owning the experience forever. And he will have been trained, back in the States with friends, in ways that are generally enjoyable. He will have been thoroughly trained to handle most of the situations he confronts. He will work with men who normally think and act as he does. He may win medals, as I did, that proclaim his courage.

And while there is no doubt about the bravery of many soldiers, sailors, and airmen under far more trying conditions than I've ever faced—especially the bravery of those facing death, of POWs—what about the woman with two kids, who doesn't have the means to take care of them, but who does so, day after day and night after night for *years?* Without training, sometimes without friendship, and without hope of help or of a Distinguished Flying Cross?

We tend to think of courage only as something shown by men in battle over a relatively short time.

It didn't take a lot of courage for me to do what I did in the war, and given the conveniences in my life, it'll probably take far less courage to raise my son than the courage shown by so many mothers and fathers in my country and around the world, in places our nation and other nations will not venture to give aid but *will* venture to make war.

When the combat flying is over for the young pilots—in any nation—who have followed me down my path, many will feel courageous, some with good reason perhaps, but only a few will grow to feel about their experience as I do now, that the pull of the flying machine, the dream of flying, seduced me.

Late in the war, I wrote in my journal a quote from somewhere: "There is no country but the heart."

A FRIEND OF MINE who lived in Vietnam after our war there wants to read this book because, having heard so much about the point of view of Vietnamese on the ground during the war, she wants to know the point of view of the pilots in the air. I've not asked her what she knows about the point of view of those on the ground. I know it's varied and complicated. But I do know that plenty of North Vietnamese and Pathet Lao troops on the ground in Laos were looking up at my airplane and thinking, I'd like to kill him. I never thought the same about them, nor do I think most of my fellow pilots were intent on killing people. Most of us were decent, good individuals who did not want to kill innocent human beings. Is an enemy soldier following his own conscience, his own family, culture, peers, and country, not innocent? Was I innocent? It's not so simple. In some ways I was, but I fear that in some ways I wasn't.

Clearly, civilians are innocent. Killing them should be seen as an unjust act—always—rather than as an "accident." And unjust acts must be, before anything else can happen, called unjust.

AND WHAT SOLDIER in the field of battle is going to admit that what he or she is doing isn't worth it? Very few, for by doing so, the soldier would have to face and admit an extraordinary stupidness in himself or herself, and as human beings we'd rather avoid that more than almost anything. And besides, no sane soldier believes that he or she will be the one to die, else enlistment would stop. It's the other guy who is going to die.

Are military people brainwashed? Is the military a cult? How is it not a cult? So overwhelming is a soldier's inclination to believe what his leaders believe that the possibility that their war might have been wrong is still incomprehensible to most veterans of Vietnam—or of any other war, anywhere. If you run the risk of dying for a cause, it may not be easy to examine the cause.

So we immunize ourselves against the deaths of innocent people—civilians and soldiers.

I hear the voices of old soldiers, old friends even, speaking to me: You're a softy. People die. War is hell.

It was never hell for me except for a short while here and there. I was just a pilot. And I loved to fly.